The Business of Love

Carlo lifted his hand and gently traced the line of her cheek. "You are too serious for the grape harvest. I will make you drunk so that you will forget you are a busy American, and you will become an amorous Italian. Then you will not mind when I do this." Bending forward, he suddenly brushed her lips with his.

A pulsing excitement filled her at the featherlike touch and the whisper of his breath across her mouth . . .

"Carlo, no," she said, pulling away, "I'm here as a professional—"

Dear Reader:

We've had thousands of wonderful surprises at SECOND CHANCE AT LOVE since we launched the line in June 1981.

We knew we were going to have to work hard to bring you the six best romances we could each month. We knew we were working with a talented, caring group of authors. But we *didn't* know we were going to receive such a warm and generous response from readers. So the thousands of wonderful surprises are in the form of letters from readers like you who've been kind with your praise, constructive and helpful with your suggestions. We read each letter...and take it seriously.

It's been a thrill to "meet" our readers, to discover that the people who read SECOND CHANCE AT LOVE novels and write to us about them are so remarkable. Our romances can only get better and better as we learn more and more about you, the reader, and what you like to read.

So, I hope you will continue to enjoy SECOND CHANCE AT LOVE and, if you haven't written to us before, please feel free to do so. If you have written, keep in touch.

With every good wish,

Sincerely,

Carolyn Nichols

Carolyn Nichols
SECOND CHANCE AT LOVE
The Berkley/Jove Publishing Group
200 Madison Avenue
New York, New York 10016

P.S. Because your opinions *are* so important to us, I urge you to fill out and return the questionnaire in the back of this book.

CRESCENDO

MELINDA HARRIS

A SECOND CHANCE AT LOVE BOOK

CRESCENDO

Distributed by Berkley/Jove

First edition published April 1982

First printing

Printed in the United States of America

Second Chance at Love books are published by
The Berkley/Jove Publishing Group,
200 Madison Avenue, New York, NY 10016

For Kathy,
who coached

CRESCENDO

CHAPTER
One

"Avanti!"

The heavily carved doors muffled the voice but could not disguise the full, rich tones of a singer. With a deep breath Alexis seized the massive brass handle and pushed open the door. She stopped, poised on the threshold, sternly commanding her pounding heart to slow down. Before her lay the library of the Villa delle Fontane Auree, and Carlo Benoni, the man who had brought her from the safety of her San Francisco travel agency to this Renaissance villa in the hills near Florence.

Oh, heavens, she murmured inwardly, what if Michael were right? What if she couldn't handle it—No! She drove the leering, whispering self-doubt into the deep secret place where she struggled to keep it locked. Amy and François had believed in her, and she was going to justify their faith. Lifting her pointed chin, she tossed back her shoulder-length black hair and stepped into the study.

Floor-to-ceiling beige drapes hung at the two windows, giving the room a comfortable shaded air. Moving further into the room, Alexis sank into a deep, chocolate-brown carpet. As her eyes grew accustomed to the dimness, she gave a small gasp, for the room was filled with books. All four walls were lined with volumes, leather-bound for the most part, their titles a gleam of gold in the shadows.

In one corner near a window stood a grand piano. Sheets of music lay scattered across the stand, and some had slipped onto the floor. It was obvious that the man who worked here enjoyed the magnificent library and chose to give it a comfortable, lived-in look.

Alexis suddenly grew aware of another person in the room. She'd been so overcome by the splendor of the library that she had overlooked the master of the villa.

But how on earth she could have was beyond her, she thought wildly as she surveyed the man who rose from behind the large mahogany desk.

She'd only seen pictures of Carlo Benoni on record jackets, in some of San Francisco's finer music stores, but they had failed to capture the sheer size and vitality of the man. He was very tall, making Alexis feel tiny, at five feet four, and in addition to his height he was... She searched for a word. Big? Massive? Certainly not fat. He was... solid.

He swept around the desk with surprising grace for so large a man, and then Alexis was enfolded in the warmth and power of the Italian singer. He happily grasped both her hands between his and beamed down at her. His lips curved into a soft smile between the dark frames of his beard and mustache. She noticed that his hands were immaculately manicured, and there was a clean, lemony scent about him, so unlike the cloying after-shaves Michael had favored. It was Benoni's eyes, however, which captured her. Deep brown, they seemed fathomless, yet their sparkling golden glints conveyed an impudent, teasing quality. As she gazed into those amazing eyes, Alexis at last understood the meaning of the phrase "windows of the soul." These windows were definitely wide open, and she liked what she saw.

"Signorina Dimitroff, Alexis." His smile broadened, and she found herself smiling in response. "I am so happy to see you. Your papa said you were *molto bella,* but he did not say enough." He stepped back and studied her admiringly. Since her divorce Alexis had felt uncomfortable when faced with frank male admiration, but for some reason Benoni's scrutiny didn't offend her. Rather she felt flattered, and slightly breathless. "I think together we are going to plan a perfect concert tour for me."

He spoke excellent English, but his lilting accent gave it a piquant charm that Alexis found irresistible. As Benoni talked, Alexis studied his sensual mouth, surrounded by the neatly trimmed beard and mustache. She was suddenly alarmed at the direction her thoughts were luring her, and, withdrawing her left hand from his grasp, she briskly shook hands.

"Thank you, Signor Benoni—"

"Carlo, please. We are going to be friends, you and I."

"All right, Carlo, and I'm quite happy to be here. I just hope my father's pride didn't mislead you into hiring me."

"No, that is not possible. Not only do you own a travel agency; you have traveled with your papa on his concert tours. I know you will make sure that I am very comfortable in New York and Boston and Washington and Chicago—"

"Please." Alexis laughed. "Don't list them all. Seeing

them in your letter was terrifying enough!" Benoni threw back his dark head and laughed with her.

The overpowering masculinity of the man was weaving its way into her being. Agitated by her deep response to the handsome singer, Alexis crossed swiftly to one of the chairs near his desk and sat down.

"Tell me, are you your father's child?" he asked, following her. "Are you also a musician?"

"Alas, no. I never had the discipline. He taught me to play piano, of course, but no"—she shook her head—"I couldn't call myself a musician."

"You like music, though? Your papa said you married a musician, no?" He leaned closer to her, over the arm of the chair, and once again the scent of his after-shave lotion swept seductively over her. The coiling tension which his nearness aroused in her, together with the mention of Michael, shook her.

"No! I mean, yes, but that's over now." Alexis leaped nervously to her feet and hurried to the piano. "This is a very beautiful instrument."

He seemed to accept her need for a change in subject, for he answered smoothly. "Thank you. It is very old. My accompanist insists on rehearsing on a fine piano, but I confess I bought it as much for myself as for Ian. It is much like this room—old, majestic, and elegant." They both paused, staring at each other across the closed lid of the concert grand. "Why don't you try it?" suggested Benoni softly.

Alexis realized guiltily that her hand had been stroking the fine grain of the wood. Quickly she snatched it back. "No, I couldn't; I haven't played seriously in years. I'd just embarrass myself and you."

"That is not possible. I see in your face that it would give you pleasure to play this instrument, and it would give me pleasure to share it with you."

His warmth and sincerity melted her resistance, and,

depositing her notebook on the piano, Alexis slid happily onto the bench. Opening the lid, she touched the keys softly, acquainting herself with their touch.

"I played a second-piano part once with my father for a small benefit concert he was doing in Carmel. California," she added hastily, noticing the bewildered look on Benoni's face. "I was about fourteen at the time, so I can't promise how much I'll remember," she warned.

"Doesn't matter," he responded, leaning comfortably against the piano.

She looked down at the keys, allowing that inner, almost muscle, memory to take control. With the first opening trill it all came back to her, the velvet feel of the night as she and her father had begun to play out on the terrace of that old house, the tangy scent of the ocean, the stars gleaming overhead, and, of course, the soft chorus of the insects which seemed to blend harmoniously with the Mozart.

Raising her head, she found Carlo's eyes devouring her face. The intensity of the look took her breath away, and her fingers faltered. She clasped her hands in her lap. "I . . . I don't remember anymore," she whispered.

"Bravo, *la mia* Alexis," he said softly. His eyes were rapt, stripping away the façade she had built, reaching that part of her which deeply regretted the teenage decision that had taken her away from music. "I think you are too critical," he continued. "You are most certainly a musician."

"And you're very kind." She paused. There was an electricity in the room, sparking between her and this powerful man, and the music seemed to be the catalyst. Alexis decided to break the too-intimate setting and return to business.

"Well, enough of this. I brought a notebook." She retrieved the small pad from the top of the piano and headed back to her haven in the leather chair. "And I thought I could start right away to get some idea of your taste in hotels, restaurants, and so forth. We also need to establish timetables and modes of travel. We'll go for an efficient blend of sightseeing and—"

"But Alexis, you must not think of working today," Carlo protested. "You have just made a long journey, and I, curious man that I am, demanded to see you first thing, instead of letting you rest. And then I make you perform for me—but no, you must rest."

"Thank you, Sig—" She stopped at the reproving look. "Carlo. But I'm really not tired. I rested in the car." There had been little else to do, she thought wryly, after her blowup with Hans Gunther, Benoni's business manager. The man had met her that morning at the airport in Pisa, and he'd made it abundantly clear he did not want his employer to make the American tour, and deeply resented Alexis' presence at the villa. They'd exchanged bitter words, and Alexis knew she'd made an enemy. The rest of the drive had passed in sullen silence. With a shiver Alexis wondered when she'd have to confront the German again, and what he would tell Carlo. Lifting her eyes to meet Carlo's, Alexis said suddenly, "I'm really anxious to get to work."

Benoni gave a deep, rolling chuckle, shaking his head. "I see you are truly an American." He crossed to where she sat, and gently brushed her cheek with a forefinger. Alexis' breath caught at the featherlike touch. "Always rush, rush, rush. But do not worry. While you are here we will teach you how to relax, to be a little more Italian."

"Signor Benoni," Alexis said, deliberately dropping the friendly "Carlo." "I didn't come here for a vacation. I have an *American* business to run, and the sooner I get back to it, the happier *I'll* be. Now I really must insist that we get to work."

She was losing control of the situation, and the feeling terrified her. She had to get started; she had to prove she could successfully do this task. Before her departure for Italy, Michael had called and warned her that she was a fool, that she lacked the brains or the expertise to handle something as complex as Benoni's tour. She still felt the same doubts that had been awakened by her ex-husband, but now added to them was the disturbing presence of her new client. Carlo Benoni was certainly not what she had counted on, and suddenly home seemed a very safe haven.

"No, *bella* Alexis," he said, calmly but firmly. "Soon I must rehearse. Then it will be time for lunch and a siesta. And as for tomorrow and Saturday, why, it is the grape harvest."

"So?" asked Alexis.

"It is a time for song and music and gaiety. You will go to the fields to join the picking, and to the winery for the pressing, and at night . . ." He flashed her a smile. "At night it is the time for dancing and drinking and"—he winked slyly—"love."

Blushing, trying to control her trembling, Alexis rose to her feet. Fury and an emotion she could not identify warred within her. Obviously Benoni cared nothing for her wishes or desires. She was just a foolish woman with a silly little travel agency. It didn't matter if she were delayed or inconvenienced, so long as he could pursue his pleasures. And how dare he take control of her life, dictating where she would go and what she would do? She had endured almost three years of such domination, and after finally escaping, she was not about to trade the old prison for a new one. And frankly, she didn't give a damn about their ridiculous grape harvest. She wanted to finish the job and go home.

"Signor Benoni, I'm not interested in your grape harvest! I find it extremely rude of you to place your pleasure above the needs of my business, but I suppose I should have expected that from an Italian male!"

Carlo gaped at her, but even his startled, comical expression could not quell her anger. She had been bossed and manipulated by Gunther earlier in the day, and now she was being laughed at and ordered about by his employer. Clutching her notebook to her chest, she said through gritted teeth, "I'm going to my room. When you decide you want to work, let me know." Whirling, she strode from the room.

The bedroom door slammed shut, sending the crystal drops on the chandelier dancing. Storming across the polished hardwood floor, Alexis flung her notebook onto the inlaid surface of the eighteenth-century writing desk. A scant thirty minutes earlier, she'd freshened up in this lovely bedroom and gone downstairs, filled with hope and fear. Now it seemed that the fear had been realized.

"He is the most irritating, infuriating, and domineering man!" she announced to the wainscoted walls. She felt better after the outburst, but her conscience pricked her, reminding her that this unfavorable view of the singer was hardly fair.

During her disastrous meeting with Benoni, someone had unpacked her case. Her pale-rose nightgown lay across the foot of the enormous canopy bed, and her cosmetics were neatly arranged on the dressing table.

She paused before a tall oval mirror and realized with chagrin that her lacy white skirt was badly crumpled. Suddenly the hours of air travel fell on her shoulders, and she sagged with weariness. A bath, she decided, was just what she needed.

She stepped into the green-and-bronze-tiled bathroom, with its shell-shaped basins and inviting sunken tub. She pinned up her hair as the bath filled, the sound of the hot, splashing water blending with the tinkle of the numerous fountains that surrounded the villa. *Villa delle Fontane Auree*. Villa of the Golden Fountains, she translated. Well, it was appropriately named. Even in this inner room, she could not escape their gurgling melody. She stripped quickly.

Sinking gratefully into the steaming, scented water, she wondered if she ought to leave. It wasn't even noon yet, and she could be back in Pisa in plenty of time to catch a trans-Atlantic flight.

And what would she say to François? She could already see the Frenchman's disapproving and disappointed blue eyes if she returned to San Francisco without meeting this challenge. Besides, she mused, thoughtfully lathering her slender arms, she couldn't do that to François and Amy. They'd stood by her and supported her in the year since her divorce, and they'd been the ones who'd encouraged her to open the agency, even joining in as partners.

World Seekers had been open only a few months, yet it was already doing well. She still couldn't believe it. And that too was a legacy from Michael. On the day they'd opened, he'd come strolling into her office, immaculate as always, and so handsome he still took her breath away.

Flinging himself into a chair, he had demanded to know "what in the hell" she thought she was doing. He'd been on tour with the San Francisco Symphony, when he'd come home to find her "wasting" his money, as he had put it.

Her mouth had gone dry at his censorious tone, and it took her several minutes to calm herself enough to realize they were no longer married. Furiously she'd told him the agency had been founded with her half of the community property, and it was therefore *her* money.

As usual, he'd ignored her, and grilled her about her employees, how much the lease had cost her, et cetera, until she'd wanted to scream. Finally he'd left her with a parting remark that he hoped she didn't go broke.

With an opening like that, was it any wonder she was still amazed when, each month, they continued to operate in the black? She'd vowed then and there that she would never again be dominated by any man, yet here she was, stonewalled, her wishes ignored, by Carlo Benoni.

With a determined expression in her clear green eyes, Alexis decided she would *not* surrender to the singer. He could eat, sleep, and party all he wanted, but she was not going to flee back to America, and she was not coming downstairs until he indicated that he was ready to work!

CHAPTER *Two*

THE BOOK DROPPED from her listless hand to lie forgotten on the green satin coverlet. She had taken lunch in her room and spent the afternoon furiously pacing the lovely suite. Nothing had helped to relieve her anger and frustration, and now, with the sun sinking swiftly in the west, it was too dark to read. She supposed she could turn on a light, but a strange lethargy had taken command of her body. Rolling over onto her stomach, she hugged a beige eyelet lace pillow and admitted she was bored.

She had spent eight hours in this lovely room, and with each passing moment it had seemed more and more a gilded prison. Benoni wasn't going to surrender and set to work as she wished, Alexis thought. What had he said about that grape harvest? Was it really two full days? Ruefully she admitted there was no way she could endure forty-eight hours trapped within these four walls. But how could she go downstairs after the scene she'd made?

Tossing the pillow aside, she slid from the bed and resumed her agitated pacing. She pushed open the French doors and stepped onto the balcony. A gentle breeze had sprung up, wafting to her the scent of wood smoke and cooking. Her stomach gave a grumble, and she realized she still hadn't solved the problem of her self-imposed imprisonment. Should she go downstairs or not?

She nibbled at her lower lip and tried to make up her mind. Before her lay the gardens of the villa. Trees stood like shadowed sentinels, and, hidden in the darkness, the fountains continued their music. The old house had been built against the side of a mountain, so over the years the owners had excavated a great amphitheater in which to plant their gardens and grottos.

"Oh, piddle," she at last announced to the night sky. "I'm not proving a thing by this. I'm only punishing myself and acting like a spoiled brat."

She ran quickly back into the bedroom. Flinging open the doors of the armoire, she surveyed her meager supply of dresses. What did one wear to dinner at an Italian villa? Finally she selected a long-sleeved, high-necked dress of peach-colored wool. She twisted her black hair into an artful knot on the top of her head, allowing a few wisps to escape at the nape of her neck and in front of her small ears. She rose and critically studied her image. The cut of the dress emphasized her slender figure, and the color brought out the delicate pink of her cheeks and lips. She hoped it was elegant enough for the occasion, and that Carlo Benoni would approve.

She was shocked at the errant thought that had slipped sneakily into her mind, and firmly banished it. She glanced at her watch. Seven-thirty. If she were going to make an appearance, she'd better get going. She squared her shoulders, pulled open the door, and stepped into the upper hall. Hurrying down the hall toward her was a young woman. Alexis was so startled at meeting someone that she almost retreated back into her room. Her cowardly flight was forestalled by a smile and a friendly wave from the dark woman. Tentatively she returned the salute.

"Allo," said the stranger brightly. "You must be Alexis."

"Yes, yes, I am."

"Carlo had been talking about you all afternoon. We were all so disappointed when you didn't come down for lunch, but I understand how tired you must have been."

"Yes. Tired," Alexis echoed dismally, feeling deceitful.

"I am Bianca, Carlo's sister."

"Of course you are!" exclaimed Alexis. "The resemblance is uncanny. I don't know how I overlooked it at first."

"Oh, please," Bianca protested with a laugh. "I hope the resemblance is not too great. I would not want to be quite as . . ." She paused, her eyes twinkling with golden lights just like her brother's, and gestured expressively to either side of her slim form. "*Grande* as Carlo."

"Oh, good heavens, no," Alexis said quickly as she looked enviously at the chic Italian woman. She wished she could appear so polished and finished in a plain tailored gray skirt and cream blouse. Perhaps it was the scarf knotted so casually at the neck, or the way her hair curled pertly about her round face, but something clearly set Bianca apart. Realizing she was staring, Alexis hurried on to add, "I was referring to your eyes. Both yours and your brother's are quite remarkable."

"Thank you, but brown can never compare with the bright green of yours."

"Oh, no," said Alexis. "There's something so warm about . . ." Suddenly both women were laughing. "Aren't we absurd?" Alexis asked, catching her breath.

"No woman is ever satisfied with what God has given her, and I suppose we are no exception," Bianca agreed.

"Well, at least we have a great mutual-admiration society going," Alexis remarked.

"Who knows; it may come in handy someday. But we will miss cocktails if we don't hurry. Come, Alexis; I will show you the way." Bianca briskly tucked Alexis' arm beneath hers. Alexis was startled at first, then remembered the European passion for walking arm in arm. She also remembered it was usually a mark of friendship and affection when someone did take your arm, and she was shyly pleased at the compliment, for she already liked the lovely Italian woman.

Bianca escorted her to a wing of the beautiful house she had not yet seen. Here the marble walls were softened with woven tapestries, and the paintings and statues were more modern, and seemed less like showpieces than elsewhere in the villa. The two women passed through double doors into an elegant salon. A small fire snapped merrily in the marble fireplace, and a number of small chairs and a satin settee were arranged about its cozy warmth. A collection of Dresden shepherdesses posed on the mantel, and overhead a crystal chandelier threw its faceted light across the room.

Hans Gunther, Alexis' nemesis, sat stiffly on one of the dainty chairs, his dark suit accentuating his white-blond hair and pale skin. His cold blue eyes slid insolently over Alexis' face as she entered; then, with a shrug, he dismissed her.

Perched on another chair, near the manager, was a small, roly-poly man with bright red cheeks and lively blue eyes. He glanced from Alexis to Gunther, who were looking daggers at each other, then leaped abruptly to his feet and rushed to hang over the back of the settee, safely out of the war zone.

"Ian, why are you acting like a frightened rabbit?" Bianca asked with a laugh. The little man blushed and hung his shaggy red head. He seemed completely tongue-tied. "Alexis, this silly little bunny is Ian McFadden. He is Carlo's accompanist."

"How do you do?" began Alexis, then faltered to a stop at the sight of the amazing figure lounging indolently on the settee. Her black dress was a masterpiece of workmanship, but the form it enfolded was nothing short of a masterpiece also. Alexis knew without being told that this was Carlo and Bianca's mother, for the lazy eyes turned to her with the same brown-gold as the children's. But there the resemblance stopped so far as Bianca was concerned. Madame Benoni possessed a bosom of truly amazing proportions, and the rest of her full figure matched perfectly.

"Mama," said Bianca, bending to kiss her mother on one round cheek, "this is Alexis Dimitroff, our American houseguest. Alexis, this is my mama, Venezia Benoni."

"Eccellente," Madame Benoni murmured huskily. "You are so welcome. Now you must sit beside me"—she extended one plump hand to Alexis, dazzling with diamond rings—"and tell me of your *caro* papa. He is a man most *simpatico,* and it has been too long since I have seen him."

"I didn't know my father knew the family," said Alexis, joining the Italian woman. Ian politely withdrew to the small portable bar which stood discreetly beneath the long row of windows. "I just assumed he and Signor Benoni were casual acquaintances."

"But no. Your papa and my Ponti were very good friends. Many nights they would spend playing this—how do you say?—ah, billiards, when Ivan was here on tour. *Ah, Dio!* But I thought I would be driven mad with the crack, crack, crack of those little balls." Alexis and Bianca exchanged amused looks; then Alexis returned her attention to the older woman.

"Where's Carlo?" Bianca asked suddenly, after consulting her watch.

"Out talking with the gardener. He's not happy with the way the trees have been pruned," Gunther answered.

"If he keeps us waiting much longer, I shall have to give the cook another raise to keep him with us," grumbled Venezia darkly.

"Don't worry, Mama. Carlo's never missed a meal yet," Bianca said with a smile.

"May I pour you a drink, ladies?" Gunther asked, keeping his eyes on Bianca.

"Thank you, Hans. I'll take a little white wine."

"And you, Miss Dimitroff? A little beer perhaps? I've been told that is the most popular beverage in your country."

"Not most popular beverage with *me*, Herr Gunther." Alexis smiled stiffly. "And I always heard your country had that honor. I'll also take a glass of wine."

Madame Benoni's sharp eyes flitted from the German to Alexis and back again. She leaned toward Alexis, apparently about to say something, when the doors flew open, and in strode Carlo.

Seeing Alexis, he crossed straight to her and took her hands in his. "You came down," he said softly. "I am so very, very glad. It was not my desire to upset you so badly this morning."

Embarrassed by his sincerity and the disturbing touch of his hands, Alexis struggled to inconspicuously free her hands from his grasp. As if sensing her agitation, Benoni quickly dropped them and turned to embrace his mother.

Venezia eyed him suspiciously. "What have you done to our guest to upset her, Carlo?" Although deep, her voice carried with great clarity to the other people in the room. Alexis felt herself beginning to blush as Gunther whirled to stare at her from where he stood at the bar.

Bianca, smiling impishly, asked, "What were you doing? Flirting again, Carlo?"

"No." The reply was short, almost terse for Carlo, and his sister gazed at him in confusion.

"Please," said Alexis desperately. "It was nothing. Signor Benoni and—"

"Carlo," he reminded her gently.

"Carlo"—she gulped—"and I just had a slight disagreement over our work schedule."

She had done a lot of thinking during the hours of her self-imposed imprisonment, and had realized that her churlish behavior earlier in the day had been directed at Michael and not at Benoni. She lifted her eyes to meet Carlo's and, taking a deep breath, said, "Carlo, I want to apologize for my behavior this morning. I . . . I didn't mean to—"

He brushed aside her words with a quick wave of his hand. "Done and forgotten," he said, smiling down at her.

"Thank heavens," Venezia exclaimed. "Dreadful boy!" She tapped him firmly on the wrist with one dimpled hand. "He is always making trouble. Usually with the cooks." She rolled her eyes expressively toward Alexis. "Three cooks he has cost us, with his demanding ways. Where was I? Oh, yes, you are disturbing the gardeners, and now you have upset Ivan's daughter."

"Don't worry, Mama. Alexis and I are reconciled now." His teasing eyes dared her to disagree.

"*Bene!* Now we may all be comfortable again."

Carlo and Bianca clustered about their mother, and the three began conversing in rapid-fire Italian. The voices grew so loud, and the gestures so broad, that Alexis feared she was witnessing a family battle. Embarrassed by her proximity to this altercation, even though she couldn't understand one word, she retreated to the far end of the room to study the paintings hung there.

"Your wine, Miss Dimitroff."

"Oh, thank you, Herr Gunther." She smiled, trying to ease some of the earlier tension that had been generated during their ride from the airport.

The manager's bleak expression didn't alter with her overture. "So you and Carlo are already having problems?" His blue eyes drilled inquisitorially into hers.

"I really feel that is a matter between my client and myself," Alexis replied stiffly.

"Maybe so, maybe so, but I think Carlo may be having second thoughts about this American tour. I think I may have made him realize your country is the haven of the great unwashed. You package and sell your performers like underarm deodorant."

The mocking arrogance of his tone and the ugliness of the remark both intimidated and infuriated her. She felt her stomach knot, and that freezing fear, a gift from Michael, seized her. No, she thought, I'm not going to remain silent. If nothing else, she owed it to her father. Summoning all her nerve, she pivoted slowly and raked the manager's thin form with cold green eyes.

"I see you're one of those Europeans who still lives in the nineteenth century. Haven't you heard, Herr Gunther? The United States has become the foremost center for the performing arts in the world. The fact that your employer has been invited to sing in my country is a compliment to him, and I think you and he should be pretty damn grateful for the chance."

The man's jaw worked furiously, but no words emerged. Seizing the opportunity, Alexis hurried down the length of the room to the still-shouting group around the settee. Even their anger seemed preferable to the cold hatred she'd just left. She felt someone looking at her, and, glancing over, her green eyes met the dancing blue gaze of the plump accompanist. He beamed at her and nodded warmly over the top of his wineglass. Then one bright eye closed in a conspiratorial wink. This evidence of one ally in the house encouraged her, and Alexis was able to still the frenzied beating of her heart.

"Bene!" shouted Carlo suddenly, and all three members of the family laughed heartily. "We have just finished the plans for the festival," he explained to Alexis. "I think you will enjoy this." He grinned.

"Do you mean to tell me the past fifteen minutes has been a discussion?" Alexis asked, astonished. "I thought all of you were about to come to blows."

"Oh no, no, *cara,*" Carlo said with a gusty laugh. He seemed about to take her hand, then apparently thought better of it. "We are just Italians. We cannot talk without yelling. That way we make sure we are heard. And our hands? Why, without our hands we would be mute."

"I think you're crazy," Alexis said, chuckling. "Here I was, being so polite and Anglo-Saxon by retreating from what I thought was a private family dispute."

"And now you find out we were just planning an outing. My poor Alexis. But now you know," he said, waving an admonishing finger under her nose. "Never, never take us seriously."

"I'll remember that," she said softly, and, with a strange, undefinable pain somewhere within her, she looked away from his handsome face.

A tiny maid pushed open the double doors and nodded brightly at Madame Benoni.

"Finalmente!" exclaimed Venezia. "Dinner at last." Heaving herself to her feet, she gathered her brilliant red shawl about her shoulders and proceeded majestically toward the doors. The river of gold chains and the large gold crucifix clinked loudly with each step. "Carlo kept

us waiting so long, I feared I would faint with hunger," she announced to no one in particular, and then she was gone, escorted by the diminutive Scot.

At her exit, Carlo and Bianca burst out laughing. "Oh, our mama," Bianca moaned, wiping her eyes.

"Faint with hunger," repeated Carlo. *"Ridicolo!"*

"But you do love her, don't you?" asked Alexis, taking the arm he offered.

"Oh, yes, little one," he murmured softly. "If I could do as well as my papa, I would be a lucky man. And so I wait, and I look, and I believe that someday there will come the woman for me." He slipped his free hand over hers where it rested on his arm and gave it a powerful squeeze. Hesitantly she lifted her eyes to meet his, and found him gazing down at her with an intent look. "Who knows, *la mia bella* Alexis, maybe she has come."

Her heart leaped, fluttering within her, and the universe narrowed to a pair of melting brown-gold eyes. *Never take them seriously. Never take them seriously,* whispered a mocking voice from her past. And the stars went out.

CHAPTER *Three*

THE MELODIOUS SPLASHING of the fountain enhanced the welcome coolness of the evening. In the two days since her arrival, Alexis had had very little time to herself, so she welcomed the opportunity to think and relax. Seated on the marble rim of the fountain's pool, Alexis admired the Renaissance simplicity and elegance of its lines. No cavorting nymphs or mermaids marred its beauty. Instead its four filigreed basins culminated in the figure of a woman gazing distantly off toward Florence.

At first Alexis had been disappointed with the gardens. The lack of flowers was alien to her American eyes, but then she had realized the "rightness" of the clipped hedges and the tall, swaying cypress trees. In the west a faint golden glow, a remembrance of the sun, still held sway, but in the east the deep blues and purples of the evening had arrived. A few stars twinkled brilliantly in the velvet darkness. With a sigh of contentment Alexis leaned over the rippling water of the pool and trailed her hand in its crystal clearness.

She shifted her position, and the layers of her petticoats crackled. She smoothed down the long red skirt with its flounce of blue embroidery and glanced self-consciously about the garden. She had slipped outside before anyone could see her. She appreciated the kind loan of the outfit but still felt ill at ease in the traditional costume. Still, if Bianca was going to wear one, she could too.

She was not accustomed to wearing hats, and the dainty red hood with its blue ribbons trailing on either side of her face gave her a very strange, tunnel view of the world. She hoped she wouldn't bump into something or someone at the festival and embarrass herself.

It had been a whirlwind two days. The first day they had gone into the vineyards surrounding the villa to join the workers. Hans had declined to accompany them, but the rest of the household, including Venezia, had gone willingly. Venezia had sat under a shade tree, waving an enormous fan languidly before her face and beaming at the people working about her. Ian, his plump face damp with perspiration, trotted to and from the large Mercedes, fetching ices, cool drinks, dainty cakes, and sandwiches—everything necessary to make her day in the fields endurable.

Carlo, Bianca, and Alexis, however, joined the local people in stripping the heavy bunches of purple grapes from the vines. At first Alexis had been clumsy, but the people around her had helped with many friendly smiles and nods, until, within several hours, she'd fallen into the rhythm.

Bianca, in khaki pants and a shirt, with her cap of black curls plastered across her forehead, laughed and joked with the workers around her. She seemed well liked and respected as the young donna of the estate, but this did not deter the younger men from flirting outrageously with her. She took their remarks and caresses in good humor, responding with a laugh and a light slap. Alexis envied her ease and confidence.

Alexis' hair had long ago fallen, and she was certain it was filled with dust and grape leaves. Michael had always insisted that she keep herself perfectly groomed—a well-dressed wife was one mark of a successful man. She wondered what he would think of her now. Secretly Alexis admitted she was glad Carlo had dragged her into participating in the harvest. As she gazed at the olive-skinned faces about her, she suddenly felt she belonged. These people's ancestors had farmed these hills for hundreds of years. Their very identities were tied to this land, yet Alexis didn't feel a stranger among them.

And then there was Carlo. Alexis tried to keep her eyes from straying too often to the row where he toiled with his people, but she found herself drawn again and again. His white shirt, now dirt-streaked, was unbuttoned to reveal his bronzed chest with its crisp, curling black hair. Each time she gazed at him, her breath caught momentarily, especially when he lifted his dark head and grinned and winked at her.

At noon all work stopped, and they gathered in the shade to eat a simple lunch of cheese, fruit, and wine. Carlo threw himself down next to her to talk and share a plate. The way his eyes lingered on the hollow at the base of her throat left Alexis trembling. She'd tried hard to avoid him, by joining Bianca or Ian, but he always managed to find her, as she secretly hoped he would.

Today had been less exhausting, for instead of going to the vineyards, they'd visited the winery. Alexis had found it fascinating to watch the baskets of grapes being poured into the great vats for pressing. Carlo had explained that the rich liquid would be drained into enormous casks and taken to the cellars for fermenting.

Carlo had taken her to visit the deep, cool cellars. They'd strolled among the casks and the racks of dusty bottles while Carlo explained the time required for the full development of each particular wine.

Alone and in close proximity with him, Alexis was again struck with the power of the man. Added to his incredible physical attractiveness were his charm and sensitivity. He listened with deep attention to everything she said. He was never abrupt or critical, unlike Michael, and Alexis relaxed more and more in his company.

"Alexis," he said suddenly, "why are you no longer married?"

The peace of the afternoon was shattered, and Alexis regarded the singer suspiciously. "I'd prefer not to discuss the subject," she stated coldly.

"Forgive me if I am being presumptuous, but your papa spoke of it, and he seems worried about you. Also I ask because you are so beautiful and I thought anyone would be a fool—"

"My private affairs are just that—private. I resent my father's discussing me behind my back; also, our professional relationship does not give you the right to pry into my life!"

She had whirled, prepared to flee, when he caught her in his arms. His brown-gold eyes gazed down into hers, filled with understanding and sympathy. "Do not be afraid, *mia cara*. To speak of it will not release the demons to plague you, I promise." A younger, more innocent Alexis longed to rest her head against his broad shoulder and pour out the fears and doubts that haunted her. But since the divorce she had built her glass wall, brick by icy brick, and now she was unable to trust him.

She had pulled from his grasp and hurried to find Bianca.

With a sigh, Alexis shook her hand dry and returned to the present. Even here in this starlit garden, Carlo's look lingered, beguiling, beckoning, urging her to trust him. She pressed her hands to her temples and wondered why she continued to snap at Carlo. Again she reminded herself not to assume every man was going to behave like Michael, but deep down she knew she didn't believe her own brave words.

"Alexis, *la mia favorita.*" It was Carlo, walking briskly along the shadowed path. When he called, there was a lyric, almost singing quality to his voice. She wondered what it would be like to hear him in concert, as she rose and shook out the folds of her skirt.

"Ah, there you are. In the darkness I almost missed you." He stared appreciatively at her. She searched his face for some hint of hurt or anger at her earlier rudeness that afternoon at the winery but found none. "You are like one of the statues come to life," he added.

"I doubt that, Carlo. I have all my clothes on."

He blinked at her, his eyes childlike and innocent. "You could take them off."

"Carlo!" But she couldn't find it in her to be offended. In fact, her heart began to hammer. To cover her confusion, she turned back to the fountain.

"I seem to be making a habit of this, but—about today," she began, her face still averted.

His hand slipped beneath her chin and turned her face to him. Releasing her chin, he placed one long finger against her lips.

"Shhhhh." For a moment they held motionless. The arm that encircled her slender waist started a molten fire coursing slowly through her veins, and Carlo delicately traced the contours of her lips with a gentle finger. Her response to his touch alarmed her, and she stiffened in his arms.

He seemed to sense her agitation, for he quickly released her. Stepping back, he said, "The others were too slow. I checked your room and when I found you gone, I thought, *bene,* she is ready, and I am ready, so we will go on together and let the others come when they will. You will walk with me, *carissima?"*

"Of course." She tucked her arm beneath his, and they began to walk toward a small hidden gate in the retaining wall. "What happens tonight?" she asked at last, deciding to break the too-companionable silence.

"Tonight is the culmination of all the labor. Tonight we dance and sing and give thanks for the good harvest and pray for another good one next year."

"This is not, I take it, a religious ceremony?" Alexis said with a teasing glance at her large companion.

He gave a shout of laughter. "Hardly. *Dio mio!* The good fathers would die of heart failure if they should attend this celebration."

"How wild is this going to be?" she asked, somewhat nervously.

"Nothing to endanger the immortal soul, and just enough to pleasure the flesh." He leered slightly. It was not a reassuring expression.

"I don't think I'm comforted," she responded dryly.

In the distance they could hear voices calling and instruments tuning. A sudden breeze carried the scent of food cooking, and Alexis' mouth began to water. They had had only a light lunch at the winery, all except Madame Benoni, of course, and it was now near seven o'clock.

The path they followed took a last climbing turn and opened out onto a large meadow. Far below and to the west twinkled the lights of Florence. Cooking fires had been lit at one end of the field, and roasting meats crackled and spit as the dripping grease fell into the fires below. Women, their long skirts covered with heavy aprons, stirred pots full of pastas and sauces.

Alexis watched as one young woman paused to pat with her forearm the beads of moisture forming on her forehead. A heavyset young man slipping up on her from behind suddenly wrapped his arms about her waist and planted a fervent kiss on her cheek. The woman's olive-skinned face lit with pleasure, and, whirling, she offered her pouting lips for a kiss.

Watching them together, Alexis felt a surge of sadness and envy. She wished she could be like these women. She had the feeling her life would be much simpler if she only had her man and her children to think of, instead of a business and her own boring problems.

"I feel I ought to be helping. They're working so hard," offered Alexis in an effort to break the depressing spiral she was falling into.

"No, no, not tonight. Tonight I am *il padrone,* and my household and I do not work."

"That seems very medieval, somehow."

"We are an old country, with old-fashioned ways. The problem is to know how much to keep and how much to replace. The *Communisti* want to change everything, but I'm afraid that would leave us all adrift, without roots in our past. On the other hand, we must not be too tied to our past. The past can be a terrible thing. Sometimes it can be like a heavy rock that people must carry with them."

Alexis shot him a suspicious look, but Carlo's eyes were on the group of men erecting trestle tables. He was right, though, she admitted to herself, and Michael was one big boulder.

"Will Herr Gunther attend tonight?" asked Alexis, and prayed that the answer would be no. Without his censorious presence, she had been able to feel a part of this warm family.

"No, I don't think so. He is a very private person, if

you know what I mean."

"You mean he doesn't like to mingle with the common people?" suggested Alexis.

"You don't like him," Carlo said abruptly.

Taken aback by the bluntness of the remark, Alexis floundered, searching for something to say. She decided only the truth would do for Carlo.

"No, Carlo, I don't like him." She hesitated, debating whether to continue. The singer's face was open, with no sign of hostility. Encouraged, she proceeded. "I don't understand why you have him around. He's so cold and critical, and you're . . . well, you're just not that kind of person," she concluded lamely.

"He disciplines me, something I will not do for myself," he explained. "He forces me to accept engagements, to work."

"But not this American tour," she protested. "He's completely against that."

"True. America was my idea."

"I wonder which he's angrier about—that you're going to cheapen yourself by going to the States, or that you made the decision without consulting him?" she mused aloud.

"A little of both, I think," Carlo admitted. "But Alexis, if he is disrespectful to you, you must tell me. I will not stand to have you insulted."

"No, don't worry about me. I'm only here for a short time, while he's your manager. You have to work with him for years to come. It's just that—" She broke off abruptly.

"Tell me," he ordered. "This is something you honestly feel, so you must speak."

"For your sake, Carlo, watch him. I'm not at all convinced he has your best interests at heart."

He lifted his hand and gently traced the line of her cheek. "You are concerned for me. That is important to me, so I will think about what you have said. But this is much too serious for the grape harvest. I am going to make you drunk so you will forget you are a busy American, and you will become an amorous Italian. Then you will not mind when I do this." Bending forward, he suddenly brushed her lips with his. A pulsing excitement filled her at the featherlike touch and the whisper of his breath across her mouth.

"Carlo," she panted, pulling away. "I'm here as a professional—"

"All the better."

"Professional *travel agent*. Let's not lose sight of our goals."

"I see my goal, and I am never going to lose sight of it, *la mia* Alexis."

She chose to ignore the burning look in his incredible eyes and the double meaning inherent in the comment.

A cheer went up from the crowd gathered in the firelight as the Benonis' big Mercedes pulled up. The door opened, and out hopped Ian, followed by Bianca, resplendent in her peasant dress and elaborate headdress. Rushing around the car, Ian held open the door as Venezia emerged. In the full-skirted embroidered costume, she was an awesome figure.

"They will wonder where I am," Carlo whispered in her ear. "Let us join them."

Without asking, he gripped Alexis' hand and led her into the pool of firelight. The cheer that had greeted the arrival of the Mercedes was nothing compared to the clamor that arose when the local people caught sight of Benoni. They swarmed about him, embracing, kissing, slapping him on the shoulder. Trapped next to the big man, much of this affection lapped over to Alexis, and she found herself greeted like a princess.

Suddenly she felt a fraud, as if she were among these people under false pretenses. After all, she was only the agent hired to plan a trip, not Benoni's consort, and not a member of this loving family. She was a stranger.

Slipping her hand from Carlo's, she began to retreat back down the mountain. Behind her a small band struck up a lively tune. Tears prickled behind her eyelids. Then she was caught by the elbow, and a gentle pressure forced her around to look up into Benoni's bearded face.

"You must not leave us, *cara* Alexis. Look!" He pointed to where a shooting star flickered across the sky. "The stars are going out because you are leaving us."

She smiled faintly at this newest absurdity but resolutely shook her head. "I . . . I can't stay. I'm not a part of this. I don't belong here," she whispered.

"In here"—his hand rested lightly on her bosom—"you know you belong. But it is this head, this busy American head, that will not release you and give you to us." He paused, his hand still lying softly over her breast. "Please, Alexis. Do not leave."

She struggled with a storm of emotions. He was wrapping her in bonds of silk, and she felt powerless to resist. She could not leave him now. Yet she was frightened, so frightened that it almost choked her. One part of her longed to surrender to this man, while another fought for escape.

She was wavering, and he saw it in her face, for he swung her up into his arms and carried her quickly back into the golden circle of fire. Her head fell against his broad shoulder, and she enhaled the clean, male scent of him. His powerful arms held her firmly against his chest as tongues of fire raced through her body.

Setting her easily on her feet, he looked teasingly down at her. "You will dance with me, *cara,* and I *will* make you drunk."

Lifting her chin, she looked him militantly in the eyes. "Is that a challenge?"

"Si!"

"This is one you can't win," she warned him.

"Alexis, I *always* win."

And she shivered, for, strangely enough, she believed him.

CHAPTER *Four*

MONDAY MORNING ALEXIS sat in Carlo's study. Her pen beat out an irritated tattoo on the arm of her chair as she waited. They had agreed to meet and begin their first work session at nine o'clock, and it was now a quarter past.

When he finally breezed in a few moments later, he bade her a cheerful good morning, but offered no apology or explanation for his tardiness. Alexis had started the day with a bad case of the jitters, but now her nervousness was overlayed with a strong sense of indignation. She briskly set a New York tour book before him, and returned to her chair.

"You liked the festival, didn't you?" he asked slyly as he flipped the pages without looking at them. His eyes were locked on her face.

"Yes, I enjoyed the festival, but I don't want to discuss it right now. We're already well behind schedule, so let's just get to work."

Chastised by her stern tone, he dropped his eyes to the page before him. Alexis knew she was good at her job, but Michael's insinuation that she couldn't handle a task as complicated as Benoni's tour hung over her, making her terribly tense.

The morning passed smoothly enough. They selected a hotel, and Alexis set up various outings and recommended several fine restaurants.

Opening a timetable book, she chose a Washington flight. "This plane leaves at 8:05 P.M. That way you can spend one extra day in New York."

"But I don't want to fly," Carlo stated calmly.

"Don't be silly, Carlo. What are you going to do, drive?"

"No, I thought I would take a train."

He had been very meek during much of the morning and had seemed content to rely upon her expertise. Now he was fighting her, and Alexis felt her jaw tighten painfully.

"The trains in America aren't very good, and besides, you'll be wasting hours."

"But I want to see the countryside."

"There is nothing to see. If this were the Colorado Rockies, that would be one thing, but this is the industrial Northeast."

"That is what you say, but maybe I ought to judge for myself."

"Are you questioning my competence?" Alexis cried, leaping to her feet, her papers and books tumbling to the floor around her.

"No, of course not. It is just that you have been making all these decisions without including me. I would like to make a few decisions for myself."

"In other words, you want to tell me what to do. Why did you even bother to hire a travel agent?"

"Maledizione!" Carlo cursed as he flung himself out of his chair. He strode forcefully about the room, and Alexis shrank back in her seat, waiting for her dismissal. She squeezed her eyes shut and felt sickened at the thought of so ignominious a return to America. Suddenly the storm passed. Carlo turned back to face her, once more smiling.

"I tell you what. Maybe we are both getting a little tired. Let us take this up again tomorrow. What do you say?"

Alexis nodded, grateful to have escaped so easily. Hastily she gathered her materials from where they had fallen, and slipped from the room.

As she stepped into the hall, she saw one of the maids busily sweeping with a small twig broom. A slow smile curved her lips as she was struck with an idea.

Crossing to the girl, Alexis pantomimed that she wanted the broom. Confused but willing, the dark-eyed maid handed it to her, and Alexis raced up the stairs with her prize. Tomorrow she would try her ploy.

"Hi," said Alexis the next morning from the door of the library. Carlo looked up from the papers before him.

He gazed suspiciously at her. "What have you got behind your back?"

"A little something to make up for yesterday."

"It is already forgotten," he replied, smiling as he pushed back his chair and came toward to her.

"Not by me," said Alexis, forcing herself to meet his warm gaze. Taking a deep breath, she pulled the small twig broom from behind her back. "Here, I'm turning in my broomstick. After all, working with a witch isn't what you bargained for."

"Ah, Alexis!" He burst into laughter, filling the room with the rich sound. Accepting the broom, he tossed it into a corner and then gripped her hands. Alexis deftly dodged the descending lips and spun out of his reach.

"Now, come on, Carlo. I did this so we could settle down and get some *work* done. It's not the signal to flirt."

"Who is flirting?" he asked innocently.

"You," she said succinctly as she planted herself in the leather chair on the opposite side of his desk. "Now, in Santa Fe I've selected the Hilton—"

"Alexis," moaned Carlo, sliding behind the desk once more, "is there nothing in America but Hilton hotels?"

"Of course there are, but the Hiltons are generally very new and quite nice."

"But, Alexis," he complained, "they are all the same. I have never been to America, and I want to see something other than McDonalds and Hilton hotels."

"Is that what you think of the restaurants I've chosen for you?" cried Alexis, stiffening without rage.

"Ah-ah." He grinned, wagging a finger at her. "Remember your new leaf." Alexis closed her eyes, groping for control. "Besides, *bella* Alexis. I am sure the restaurants are all *perfetto*. And I am sure I will love them and become even stouter than I already am."

"You are *not* stout," Alexis snapped with exasperation.

"No, of course not. You are right, my darling," Carlo answered humbly, lowering his eyes and giving a very credible imitation of the henpecked male. In spite of herself, Alexis' laughter came bubbling up.

"Oh, Carlo, you're impossible. Okay, since you don't like Hilton hotels, let's see what else we can find." She handed him several tour books for Denver and Santa Fe.

As Carlo flipped through the brightly colored pages, Alexis leaned back in her chair and surreptitiously studied her client. He had rolled back the sleeves of his shirt to bare his muscular forearms, and as Alexis watched the play of muscles and tendons beneath the smooth skin, she suddenly remembered the past Saturday night when Carlo had carried her in his arms. An unaccustomed warmth spread through her, and she knew she was blushing.

"Now, look. Here is something called La Posada. That looks nice, and it is close to downtown Santa Fe."

"Let me see," Alexis said, reaching across the desk. She quickly scanned the half page of information, then smiled at Carlo. "You're right. It looks lovely, and you'll really be able to get the flavor of Santa Fe. Now, about places to dine. Let me recommend the Compound or the Pink Adobe."

She rose from her seat and perched on the edge of the desk, crossing her legs. Carlo leaned forward, and together they scanned the pages devoted to the restaurants of the old New Mexican city. Glancing over, Alexis traced with her eyes the line of his throat and jaw. His dark head was so near, she had an overwhelming urge to reach out and stroke the silky darkness of his hair. Sternly she banished the desire and returned to the book.

An hour later Alexis flipped shut her notebook and glanced at her watch. "Almost time for lunch. I guess we'd better call it quits for today."

Carlo deftly swept together the papers littering the desk. "If you are not busy this afternoon, my *bella* Alexis, I would like to invite you to sit in on my rehearsal with Ian."

"Really?"

"Yes, why do you sound so surprised?"

"Well, my father has never liked to practice with

anyone in the room. He says he feels like he's giving a performance and can't correct any problems he may be having."

"Oh, I don't worry. I just sing, and if I make a mistake, I sing it again. If you promise not to laugh at me . . ." he said teasingly.

"As if I would. What time should I be here?"

"Two o'clock."

"All right, I'll see you then."

"What about lunch?" Carlo asked. "Won't you be there?"

"Bianca is packing some sandwiches, and we're going to explore the gardens a bit."

"Well, maybe you should have some male protection," he began hopefully.

"No," came a laughing voice from the doorway. "This is a time for girl talk, and I want a chance to get to know Alexis without your hovering around like a big bear."

They both turned to see Bianca standing in the door swinging a basket. "Come, Alexis, before he wheedles his way in with us."

"Is he good at that?" asked Alexis with a teasing glance over her shoulder at Carlo.

"*Very* good. Now, stop looking so despondent, Carlo, and go eat your lunch."

"Food for the body is no substitute for food for the soul." He sighed.

"So go pray." Bianca laughed. Carlo let out an inarticulate growl as his sister grasped Alexis' hand and led her from the library.

Alexis leaned back against the grassy hillside and sighed with contentment.

"You are feeling more at ease here now, no?" Bianca asked.

"Yes, I really am." She gave the Italian woman a

rueful look. "Was it so obvious how painfully nervous I was?"

"Only to Carlo, I think. He is very sensitive and perceptive. He spoke to me on Monday about you. I hope you don't mind, but he wanted us to find a way to put you at ease."

"I suppose I should be resentful being discussed behind my back, but I know your interest was well meant, so I won't be snappy." Alexis pulled off another handful of purple grapes and bit slowly into the sugary fruit.

A question had been tormenting her ever since the festival on Saturday night, and she weighed whether to ask it. Finally she decided to try. Tossing aside the now-bare twig stripped of its succulent grapes, she sat up, gripped her knees, and squarely faced Bianca.

"Why hasn't Carlo married yet?" she blurted inelegantly.

"I think he looks for too much," Bianca responded slowly. "He doesn't want some polished jet-setter who only wants to party and who would view him like some kind of prize. A family is very important to him, and he wants a home and children."

"Then why not marry your version of the girl next door?"

"I think he is looking for a little more spice in a wife, and not just in the spaghetti sauce. We Italians tend to be a bit demure and obedient, and I think Carlo likes a challenge."

"But surely, with all the traveling he does, and as popular as he is, he would have met someone by now."

"Would you want to marry an adoring 'fan,' or someone who loves you for yourself—the man, not the star?" Bianca asked wisely.

"I see your point." Alexis dropped her chin on her knees, considering what she had heard.

"Why do you ask? Are you looking for the position?"

Carlo's sister teased gently.

"Bianca! Of course not! I mean, we scarcely know each other, and after my first disastrous attempt, I'm not about to rush back into anything."

"You were married?" Bianca asked incredulously. "When? What happened?"

"Good grief, look at the time," exclaimed Alexis, glancing suddenly at her watch. "I promised Carlo I'd sit in on his rehearsal, so I'd better hurry." Standing, she shook out her plaid skirt and picked up the basket.

"You're evading the issue," accused Bianca.

"You're damn right I am," Alexis answered with a laugh, and she was surprised she could laugh over a subject that had held her in a painful vise for seven months. "Look, sometime I'll tell you about it, but not right now." And she realized that she wasn't lying. Sometime she really would talk with this new friend.

They hurried back to the house. Bianca took the basket and darted in the kitchen door, while Alexis crossed the marble veranda and slipped through the French doors into the library.

Carlo hadn't arrived yet, but Ian was there, straightening piles of music with quick, nervous gestures.

"Hi," said Alexis, and felt immediately bad for having startled the little man. He gasped and dropped a handful of xeroxed sheets, which went floating about the room.

"I'm sorry." Alexis moved to him and, dropping to her knees, helped him gather up the scattered pages.

"Oh, not to worry," he said with his soft Scottish burr. "I get a bit woolly just before I play."

"Woolly?" asked Alexis, puzzled.

"You know, I wool-gather a bit."

"We haven't had much of a chance to get to know each other," Alexis added, anxious to keep the conversational ball rolling. From her first night at the villa, she'd sensed she had an ally in the small redhead, and she didn't want to lose the advantage.

"Well, we each have our job, and it is a big house," he responded noncommittally.

"You sound like you're dodging everyone."

"No, only a certain someone." He raised one eyebrow, and Alexis knew he was referring to Gunther.

"How did you come to play for Carlo?" she asked, deciding not to push the little Scot to reveal any confidences.

"Let me go around the barn a bit to answer that, all right?" She nodded. "I hate to play solo, but at the Edinburgh Festival six years ago I was forced into it. Carlo was in the audience, and after the performance he came back to talk with me. He told me I'd looked miserable out on the stage, and I found myself telling him all my fears and doubts about my future as a pianist. Sounds strange that I would open up like that to a total stranger, but you know Carlo. Anyway, he asked me to play while he sang, and he hired me on the spot. I left solo work with nary a backward glance, and I've never regretted it."

"I'm not used to that kind of an attitude toward accompanying. I guess it's the result of being raised by a concert pianist, but my dad's always hated to accompany."

"Aye, I know. Two years ago I became ill in Vienna. Your father was there, and, their being old friends, Carlo decided he would play the recital. It was a disaster."

"For them or for the audience?" Alexis laughed.

"Them, I think. Your father was expressing and interpreting the music in his way, and Carlo was interpreting it in a different way, and apparently it was a bit like a one-legged man dancing a waltz. The audience must have known something was up, though, for I understand Carlo and your dad were gazing daggers at each other."

Alexis chuckled, picturing her normally serene, gray-haired father glaring at Carlo over a grand piano.

"I thought you weren't going to laugh at me, and here you are laughing already," Carlo accused her. She and Ian whirled, startled by the singer's quiet entrance.

"I'm laughing about my father," said Alexis with dignity, "and I'm getting to know Ian."

"A worthy pastime." Carlo clapped the smaller man on the shoulder as he took his position by the piano. "Now, you sit there"—he pointed to the desk chair—"and Ian and I will begin."

"What would you like to start with?" murmured Ian.

"Tamino's first aria. But first a little warm-up."

Carlo rested his hands on the polished surface of the piano and, closing his eyes, began to vocalize. The scales fell like liquid crystal from his bearded lips. From simple one-octave scales Carlo switched to octave leaps, trilling and holding the top note. Alexis watched with fascination as Ian's slender hands crept inexorably up the keys. A sharp, B, high C, high *D!* Alexis felt a constriction in her throat, and her head seemed to vibrate from the shimmer of the sound. Now she understood why the tenor was often called the most exciting range of the human voice.

Several minutes later, after Carlo had made what sounded to Alexis very much like bird calls, and darted up and down the scale with a bright, clear stacatto, he gave a grunt of satisfaction and slowly flexed his hands.

Opening his eyes, he cocked an inquiring glance at Ian. "How about that? She didn't laugh during that part, so I suppose I am safe. What do you think?"

"I think you're safe," Ian agreed with a shy smile. "If she can control herself while you honk like a goose, I think she will last through the rest."

"Will you stop talking about me as if I'm not present?" complained Alexis. "Carlo, I've told you over and over I'm not going to laugh. I don't know how you ever became a performer—"

He began to chuckle as he stared impudently across at her. Alexis dropped her face into one hand and in a muffled tone said, "Why do I fall for it every time? Carlo, you're a big tease."

"La mia Alexis, you are so pretty when you are being so intense and sincere."

"Thanks," she said sarcastically, more than a little disgruntled. "I'll remember that next time you're in need of sympathy."

The singer's face fell comically. "Oh, you would not be so heartless—"

Ian cleared his throat pointedly and glanced down at the glowing red numerals blinking on his wristwatch. Carlo shrugged guiltily. "Now you see why I need Gunther, eh?" he stage-whispered to Alexis. He clapped his hands together and in resonant tones exclaimed: *"Sbrighiamoci!* We begin."

Since she was a pianist, Alexis first watched Ian McFadden, as he tenderly touched the keys in the opening chords of the aria. His round, freckled face became almost beautiful as he poured himself into the music. There was the slightest pause, then into the hush of the afternoon floated the pure tones of Tamino's love song from Mozart's *Magic Flute*.

Even though Alexis' father had been primarily interested in piano music, he had not neglected the rest of his daughter's musical education. She had attended operas in most of the great houses of Europe and America, and the librettos of many were as familiar as old friends. This opera was no exception.

Carlo had turned away from the piano to face her as he sang, and the look in his eyes made her breath catch.

He held up both hands as if capturing her image in his mind's eye, and his voice continued to caress her senses.

At first Alexis was too shaken with the power and majesty of his voice to be aware of the words, but at last they wove into her consciousness. A cool summer's night at the Santa Fe Opera, high in the mountains of northern New Mexico, came back to her. She remembered how she and her father had cuddled beneath a wool blanket, for the evenings were cool in this outdoor amphitheater, while his long finger had indicated in their well-worn libretto book the translation of the aria that Carlo now sang.

It was as if the years had never intervened. The words rose to her mind, and she read them as clearly as she had that night so long ago.

This portrait is bewitchingly fair, such as no eyes have ever seen! I feel that this divine picture fills my heart with a new emotion. This something I cannot name; but I feel it here burning like fire. Can this sensation be love? Yes, yes! It can only be love. Oh, if only I might find her! What would I do? I would press her to my ardent heart, and make her mine forever.

Alexis' green eyes were caught in the golden web of Carlo's, and she felt as if she were being embraced by him. The aria was sung for her, and its passion surged over and through her, seeking to warm her, sweeping away her fears. She wondered dreamily what it would be like to share Santa Fe with Carlo. She would rest her head on his shoulder and gaze up at the stars glittering beyond the sweeping beams of the stage. Instead of a blanket, his arms would serve to warm her.

But there was one icy center of her that could not be warmed even with her dream. From within this frozen fortress Alexis gazed longingly out at the promise of love Carlo held so tantalizingly before her. But she was trapped, unable to cross the numbing walls that surrounded her.

Damn you, Michael, she thought. What had he done to her? Or had she done it to herself? And that thought was a terrifying one, for this self-imposed imprisonment would be harder to escape than if her jailor were outside herself.

CHAPTER
Five

"WHERE DO WE go today?" Carlo seated himself on the edge of the desk and looked at Alexis with anticipation. The rehearsal had ended, and Ian had quietly closed the door behind him, leaving the two of them alone. In the past four days, since Carlo had first invited her to stay for rehearsal, Alexis and the singer had spent every afternoon together. Today looked to be no different, and though she loved to be with Carlo, Alexis was beginning to feel a bit closed in.

"I," Alexis said, stressing the singular pronoun, "am going to the Baptistery of San Giovanni, and to see the David."

"Bene. You have your little book again," Carlo said

accusingly, glancing down at the slim volume tucked beneath her arm.

"Yes. Tour books are useful. That's why I brought so many for *you* for your American tour."

Oh, *si,* I agree. But!" He held a finger under her nose. "Why do you need a book, when you have me?"

"Carlo, I really appreciate all the time you've devoted to me, driving me through the hills and taking me into Florence, but isn't there something else you ought to be doing?"

"I am being an attentive host to my guest."

"But I'm *not* your guest!" Alexis said, exasperated. "I'm your travel agent. I work for you. You pay me. Remember?" She felt a sudden stab of guilt. Work? Well, that was debatable. The longest she had kept Carlo at their task was a mere two hours.

"You will like the David," said Carlo conversationally as he pulled the book deftly from her grasp and tossed it into the wastebasket next to the desk.

"Carlo!" But it was no use. Benoni was as ruthless as the tide, and just as all-embracing. With her arm tucked firmly beneath his, he pushed open the library doors and led her into the entryway. Before they reached the front doors, they were caught by Gunther calling urgently from the stairs.

"Herr Benoni, *bitte!*"

Carlo revolved slowly to meet his agitated manager. Two hectic spots of color burned on the German's thin cheeks.

"Surely you're not going out again."

"But of course," Carlo responded gaily.

"I told you yesterday we had to discuss these concert bookings."

"Oh, *si,* I remember. Ah, well, it will just have to wait. Tomorrow, tomorrow I promise we will deal with it."

"Carlo, if you need to work, that's all right. I can get into the city on my own." Alexis rushed into the ominous silence that had fallen after Carlo's words.

She didn't want Gunther angry with the singer, and she also saw a way to escape from Benoni's disturbing presence, since lately Carlo had been insisting on accompanying her on her rambles through the lovely Renaissance city and its surrounding hills. One traitorous little part of her reveled in the attention lavished upon her, but her practical side warned that the Italians were famous flirts and the anticipation with which Alexis met each day was dangerous.

She was giddy with excitement whenever she was with Carlo, and she found herself welcoming the end of their work sessions so they could explore together. But she could not forget that Carlo himself had warned her never to take him seriously. And there was also the fact that he was not the sort of man Alexis wanted to become involved with. He was far too powerful and commanding, and she had vowed she was never going to be controlled again. Still, it was hard to equate the joking, lusty Carlo with her tense and opinionated ex-husband. Her thoughts flew in confused circles as she waited for Carlo's answer.

Benoni smiled a bit coldly at his manager, and his grip on Alexis' hand tightened. "Now, Gunther," he said, "don't be a tin soldier. It makes no difference whether we discuss the concerts today or tomorrow, and now Florence is calling." He grinned at Alexis, his teeth very white against the dark frame of his beard and mustache.

The manager muttered something under his breath and strode away down the hall. Alexis felt a sinking sensation, for it seemed she never came in contact with Gunther without irritating him. Carlo seemed oblivious to those currents of anger and tension, and simply hurried her to the car.

They passed the twenty-minute drive into the city in a silence which even Carlo seemed disinclined to break. When Alexis stole a look at him, there was a small furrow between his arched brows. Idly she wondered what he was like when he was angry, and then decided that was a bit of information she could do without. She had the feeling that beneath all his joviality was a very strong man who was very used to getting his own way and who would probably be terrifying if roused to anger.

As they drove in from the hills, the traffic became increasingly hectic, and Alexis involuntarily closed her eyes. She opened them quickly, however, for she loved the panorama of the beautiful bridges of Florence spanning the Arno River, and the lofty cupola of the cathedral, which dominated the skyline. The big Mercedes purred down the Via Ricasoli toward the Piazza del Duomo. Alexis flinched several times as Carlo blasted through the speeding traffic around them.

"You're not used to my driving yet?" he asked innocently, looking at her out of one eye.

"A person couldn't get used to it in a lifetime," she responded tartly.

"Well, we will just have to keep practicing, what do you say, *bella* Alexis?"

"Have I got any choice? You keep kidnapping me every day."

"I want you to have a good time, and you know what they say. . . ." He paused and looked significantly at her.

"All right." She sighed, giving in to the game. "What do they say?"

"All work and no play makes Alexis a terrible lover."

Her cheeks were burning, but she looked him in the eye. "You know what else they say?" she asked sweetly. He looked at her a bit suspiciously and shook his head. "All play and no work makes Carlo a boring lover."

"Do you want to see how boring?" he asked as they pulled into a parking space. Alexis leaped from the car before he could move to the other side to help her. The last thing she needed after their flirtatious exchange was the touch of his hand. She was already too physically aware of him.

"Which way, Tonto?" she asked brightly.

"Who is Tonto?"

"A famous Indian scout who guided the Lone Ranger in their travels."

He considered the concept, then nodded and smiled. "Yes, that is me. Only, I would rather be known for guiding people astray."

"I'm sure you don't have to worry about earning that reputation. Now lead on."

"The baptistery is there." He pointed across the square at the octagonal building decorated with columns and round arches with dividing lines of green and white marble.

"The baptistery was built around the year one thousand," Carlo explained as he guided her across the *piazza*. "It has been added to over the years, but basically it is very much as it was when Dante was baptized there."

"The doors are the real attraction, though, aren't they?" Alexis asked.

"Indeed, yes," Carlo agreed. "And we will take them chronologically," he added as he led her to the south side of the building.

They paused before the massive bronze door with its twenty panels depicting stories from St. John. "This door was done by Andrea Pisano in the fourteenth century. It does not receive as much praise as the other two, done by Ghiberti, but I will let you judge which you prefer."

Alexis was again amazed by Carlo's almost encyclopedic knowledge. In their four days of exploration, she had never seen him at a loss for a story or a bit of history to enliven the beautiful objects and buildings they had seen.

"You really love this city, don't you?" she asked softly

as they moved on to the east and north doors.

"Oh, yes. It is my city. I was born here, and she fills me. I think I drank art and music from her, and now . . ." He paused, and shrugged self-conciously. "And now I try to pour back some of that which she gave me."

Gazing up into his amazing eyes, Alexis felt a deep tenderness for this sensitive, boisterous, and powerful man. Forgotten were the arguments over timetables, and the fact that he had taken over her life ever since her arrival. She ached to touch the soft skin of his cheek above the beard.

Carlo stared at her ardently, and she lost herself in the liquid darkness of his eyes. Her breath came in short pants as he lifted his hand, almost cupping her cheek. Her skin tingled in anticipation of the touch. Then, shatteringly, the church bells across the city rang out, sounding the hour. They leaped apart. Embarrassed, Alexis thrust her hands deep into the pockets of her safari pants suit and turned to the final Ghiberti door.

"Ah . . . ah, as you can see," Carlo said, trying to return the day to the easy joking level they had earlier shared, "the style is much different on this door, dating, as it does, from the fifteenth century. Ghiberti devoted the second half of his life to completing this masterpiece." He shook his head, bemused. "I cannot understand giving so much time to an object. A person, now, that is different."

Alexis shot a quick glance at her companion, but his eyes were fixed on the burnished patina of the door. He seemed to sense the confusion his words had created in her, for he didn't take her hand or arm when they began walking to the Galleria dell'Accademia. Instead they walked side by side, with their hands in their pockets.

This was Alexis and Carlo's first journey into the heart of the city, and suddenly Alexis realized that they were attracting a great deal of attention. Women beamed at

Carlo and surreptitiously smoothed their sweaters and adjusted their hose. Around them the whispers ran like rain over pebbles. *Benoni, l'illustre*. Nor was Alexis immune from the excitement. She too was obviously the source of much speculation, and even of good-natured ogling from the men.

A crowd was gathering, following discreetly, anxious to approach him but shy and uncertain. Carlo kept turning back to smile and wave at the throng of people, mostly women, who stalked them. Alexis felt resentment gnawing at her. This was her time with Carlo, and she wanted no intrusions.

At the Accademia, Carlo paid for their entrance into the museum, and they made their way quickly to the vast circular room which housed Michelangelo's David. The murmur of the crowd was left behind in the marble stillness of the room, and Alexis felt the muscles in her neck and back relax. She knew her reaction to the admiring group was irrational, but she couldn't quell it. This sort of adoration was acceptable at the stage door after a concert, but not in the street. She pushed the thought of the crowd from her mind and turned her attention to the magnificent statue before her.

The David towered over her, more than fourteen feet in height. She felt almost crushed by the sheer size and power of the figure. As she became accustomed to the heroic proportions of the youth gazing forever at his enemy, with somber eyes, Alexis was able to appreciate the detail that Michelangelo had devoted to his masterpiece. She stared in amazement at the etched tendons that ran from the wrist to the right hand.

She was shaken and overcome by the presence of such genius, and it left her feeling small and insignificant. She stole a glance at Carlo, who stared with smiling admiration at the statue. His arms were folded across his barrel chest, and Alexis' eyes lingered on the outline of his muscles and shoulders under the soft jacket. He too seemed as heroic as a Renaissance sculpture, and Alexis savored the powerful lines of his body.

He suddenly became aware of her eyes on him, and with a sigh he stretched and moved to her. He was very close, and she felt the warmth emanating from him in the cold of the marble room. There was a fluttering in her stomach, and she felt the slow, sensual tightening of the muscles in her lower back as his warm breath blew like a feather on her face. She swallowed convulsively and stepped back out of the magic circle that seemed to surround him.

"You're blushing," he said teasingly.

"No, I'm not!" But her hand flew to her cheek.

Carlo reached out and captured her slender fingers. His thumb casually stroked her fingers, and she trembled. "What's the matter?" he asked, grinning wickedly down at her. "Is it the lack of a fig leaf?"

Her eyes flew guiltily to the statue behind them, and for the first time she became aware of the complete nudity of the figure.

"Carlo!" she gasped. "This is great art," she sternly lectured him, "not pornography. And I'm not some little-old-lady school teacher who is shocked by the human body."

"I'm so glad," he murmured as his lips brushed softly across her hair. Her senses raced at the featherlike touch, and she lifted her face expectantly.

"Harold, *will* you look at this-here statue?" Carlo and Alexis leaped away from each other as an enormous woman, swathed in a loud print tent dress, descended upon them. Trotting obediently behind her was a small, roly-poly man who smirked at the couple and never even glanced at the masterpiece before him.

The woman's bellowed remarks echoed about the domed room, and Carlo winced. "I think we'll go now," he whispered to Alexis. Gripping her hand, he pulled her from the Accademia.

"Ah, *Dio!*" he exclaimed, flinging his hands up. "Are all Americans like that?"

"I'm an American. Am I like that?" replied Alexis, stung by his comment.

"No, of course not. You are special."

Alexis brushed back a strand of hair that had fallen from her chignon, and sighed. "I didn't mean to be so touchy, Carlo. Unfortunately, many times the Americans who have the money to travel also have no taste."

"And I did not mean to be so critical of your countrymen," Carlo said contritely. "We complain about Americans more out of habit than anything else. But I think your people are very vibrant and interesting. That is why I want to make the tour."

"It won't do your career any harm either," Alexis noted dryly.

"That is true."

Carlo pushed open the door of the palace. They stepped into the crisp September air and were besieged. A crowd of fifty or sixty women waited on the narrow sidewalk and spilled into the street. Alexis was swept from Carlo's side in the rush of femininity that sought to be close to him. Italian chirped, bubbled, and thrilled on all sides of her, as the women, like gaily plumed birds, flocked to the singer.

They waved autograph books frantically, and Carlo, laughing good-naturedly, pulled a pen from a pocket inside his jacket. A beautiful young woman, her hair an ebony waterfall, advanced provocatively on Carlo. He eyed her appreciatively and, after signing her book, slipped an arm around her slender waist and firmly kissed her. A great cheer went up from the crowd, and Carlo bowed and saluted them with an amazing blend of charm and arrogance.

Alexis stood forgotten, with her back pressed against the rough surface of the palace wall. A pretty blond woman, a typical northern Italian, slipped up behind Carlo and deftly pulled his handkerchief from his coat pocket. There was a shriek of jealousy from the others as the petite blond slipped through the crowd waving her trophy gleefully over her head. Carlo clutched his jacket about his body and continued to flirt and joke.

Alexis' emotions roiled within her. Bleakness and anger struggled for supremacy, and she felt hot tears pricking at her eyelids. Furiously she brushed away the betraying wetness. What had come over her? she wondered. Was she jealous? But a person had to be involved to be jealous, and she certainly wasn't involved with Carlo Benoni. *Liar,* whispered an evil little voice. *You want him, and you hate it when he forgets your presence.* Alexis felt battered by the conflicting emotions that beat through her mind and body. She couldn't bear to watch Carlo in the midst of the cooing, caressing throng; whirling, she strode away from the noisy scene.

You can't walk away from it forever, persisted the voice. *Sooner or later you're going to have to face it.*

Face what? she thought bitterly. Carlo Benoni was more trouble than he was worth, and she, unlike all the others, wasn't going to be lured by his glib tongue and charming ways. After all, the Italian national pastime was flirtation, and she was not about to be suckered by that. Not after what she'd just been through with Michael. The thought of her ex-husband made a bad day worse, and, shivering in the suddenly sharp breeze, Alexis wrapped her khaki jacket tighter about herself as she continued to walk back to where they had left the car.

"Alexis!" The shout echoed down the winding street. Resolutely she increased her pace. She heard running footfalls behind her. The primal terror of pursuit and capture filled her, and she almost broke into a run in

response. Suddenly she realized what a ludicrous picture they both must present, and came to an abrupt halt.

He was panting when he joined her, and his hair was tousled, giving him a little-boy look. "Why did you run from me?" he demanded, gripping her shoulders. His eyes were dark with concern.

"I didn't . . . I wasn't . . ." She gestured helplessly, searching for the words, then hung her head. "I don't know."

"Do not run away, Alexis." He pulled her closer to his chest, his breath puffing warmly onto her upturned face. His arms held her strongly. His chest rose and fell against her bosom, and she was pressed against the warm length of his body. An answering warmth grew in her lower limbs and coiled swiftly upward through her. Her slender form seemed molded to him, and she savored the sweet glow that his touch excited in her.

"You can't ever run away, you know," he added softly. "I will always find you and take care of you."

The arrogance of his words infuriated her. Outraged, she shook loose from his embrace.

"Do *not* tell me what I can and cannot do!" Her eyes blazed with green fire. "I will not have it from you or anyone else. You men," she said, gesturing disgustedly. "You see a woman who is mature and capable and out on her own, and immediately you assume she's pining away because she doesn't have a male to protect her. Well, disabuse yourself of the notion, Carlo. I didn't start my own company and make it a success by folding my hands and waiting for some man to do it for me!"

"I am not certain how we got on this subject." Carlo spread his hands helplessly. "You were upset because of the women, I know that."

"You're assuming a lot," she said, her voice tight.

He glared down at her. "I am going by what my eyes tell me. You were jealous. What you must try to understand is that it was just flirting."

"Oh, don't worry, Carlo. I've become an authority on flirting, since I've met you. Now I would like to return to the villa. I'm afraid Florence has lost its charm for me!"

Closing her notebook with a snap, Alexis gathered up her materials. Carlo leaned back in his chair and laced his fingers across his stomach. "You're not going to stay for rehearsal?"

"No."

"Please, do not shut me out, Alexis." He paused. "We had a little fight, but it is nothing. Can you not trust me? Ever since yesterday you have been so distant." He was serious now. The banter was gone.

She chose her words carefully, not wanting to get back into the futile, circular argument. "Nothing is the matter, Carlo. Bianca and I are going into the city to shop, so I'm not staying for rehearsal."

"What are you shopping for?"

"Gloves. Bianca tells me Florence is famous for leather."

"That is true, but Bianca has no more sense than a flea. She will take you to all the wrong places. Better *I* should go with you." He tapped his chest proudly with one finger.

"You have to rehearse." Her friends would have recognized the danger signals from her flat, low tones. But they were not here to warn him, and Alexis was ready to fight, and not about to inform him.

"So today, I just don't rehearse. No problem, eh?" He leaped to his feet and beamed at her.

"*Yes,* problem. I don't want you to come. I want to go shopping with your sister."

"But I am much more interesting than my sister." He was obviously trying to jolly her, to joke her back into good humor, as he had done before. But Alexis was still too close to the scenes in Florence the day before to be beguiled. He was too strong, too powerful. It would be so easy to love him, and then she would be lost. If ever she gave herself to him, her hard-won independence would be gone. And yet she wanted him with an almost desperate longing. She pushed aside the disquieting desire and concentrated on the arrogant way he had assumed he could mold her life. Her anger was a bitter taste on the back of her tongue.

"That's debatable," she said through gritted teeth.

He drew back as if she'd hit him. She knew what she was doing was wrong, but she feared that unless she acted, there would be no escape. If she were to elude his seductive power, she had to act now, or she would never remain her own person. Holding to that thought, she allowed her evil genuis to goad her on.

"I want you to leave me alone. I'm here to plan your tour. What I do on my own time is my business, and that's the way I want to keep it. If I'd wanted a tour guide, I'd have hired one!"

She spun on her heel and started for the door. His powerful hands closed on her upper arms, and he forced her around to face him. She steeled herself to meet his anger, but, to her surprise, the dark eyes were kind. Releasing her, he ran his hands through her heavy mane of hair.

The touch of his hands against the sensitive skin of her neck was like fire and ice. Alexis longed to feel his arms about her and yearned for him to crush his lips against hers, rather than give her the flirting little kisses he'd bestowed on her thus far.

"You are afraid," he murmured against her ear. "I understand that, and I can wait."

She seized his hands and pulled them away from her. "I am not afraid, Carlo. I admit you're a very charming and attractive man, but you're no good for me. You're far too dominating, and I've been through all that and have grown beyond it."

"You think you know your heart," he argued, "but you are allowing your decisions to be colored by the past. You are not giving me a fair chance."

"Carlo, I'm here in a professional capacity. If I become more interested in Carlo the man than Carlo the performer, I'll be cheating you. I think it best if we get back on a more businesslike footing. I'll see you at dinner."

She reached the door and pulled it open. Behind her Carlo called gently, "Alexis, I am not giving up, you know. You are *il mia tesoro.*"

My treasure. Even her feeble Italian was good enough for her to be able to translate the words. She trembled, trapped between her desire to stay and the belief that she was correct and should put some distance between Carlo and herself. At last she broke the stasis that held her and stepped resolutely through the door.

CHAPTER
Six

SHE HELD THE plaid skirt against her body and studied the effect in the mirror. Frowning, she tossed the garment onto the bed, where it joined the sad pile of already-discarded outfits. The job of planning Carlo's tour was taking longer than she had anticipated, and after more than a week in Florence, her slender wardrobe was looking a trifle tired. How many times had she trotted out her six dresses and three pants outfits? Too many, she decided. Something, something positive, had to be done.

The past few days, since her confrontation in Carlo's arms, had been uncomfortable. Alexis had pasted back together her professional shield and taken refuge behind it. She had worried that Carlo might try to break through her defenses and attempt to recapture the growing intimacy they had shared, but he had remained quiet and withdrawn during their work sessions.

For Alexis, at least, this new Carlo was much more difficult to deal with then the jocular one. In spite of her decision to remain aloof, she was still fantastically aware of him physically. But without the joking, there was no way to expend the sexual tension that continued to mount between them.

With a sigh she crossed to the bed and selected a pair of white pants and a soft yellow silk shirt. Dressing quickly, she ran a brush through her hair and started downstairs to meet with her client.

Halfway down the long, curving staircase, she met Bianca, who bounded up the steps two at a time. Her cheeks were red with exertion, and her eyes were shining with excitement.

"Alexis!" she said with a gasp, then paused for air.

"Bianca, what is it? Is something wrong?" She took the younger woman's shoulders, alarmed at Bianca's urgency.

"We are going to Rome. *All* of us."

"What?"

"Si, it is true."

"But I don't understand. I mean, I have work, and . . ." Alexis' voice trailed off in confusion.

"Carlo is to sing with the Rome Opera in *Un Ballo in Maschera*. And instead of going just with Gunther, he had decided it would be much more *ameno*—how do you say?—ah, pleasant, if we all went. But I must prepare. I have nothing to wear," she wailed as she rushed off up the stairs.

Alexis reached for her, but it was too late. The lovely Italian was gone. Step by slow step, Alexis descended the stairs, her thoughts in turmoil.

She was beginning to see the end of this gargantuan

task. They'd selected hotels in most of the fourteen cities of Carlo's tour, and they were now working out the details of transportation and various outings so that he could get the flavor of the United States.

With the end so near, the vision of home beckoned, and not because of her business or because her friends were there, but because it was a haven of safety and security away from the disturbing presence of Carlo Benoni. Now she was to be delayed yet again, and the consequences of spending more time in Italy terrified her. Carlo had begun to invade her sleeping as well as her waking thoughts. She found herself constantly reliving the feel of his arms around her and the golden warmth of his touch.

Carlo's voice, gaily singing, floated through the open door of the library. Alexis entered to find him flipping through music books. He returned some to the piano, but he dropped most of them into the voluminous old briefcase that rested on the floor at his feet. The room was electric with his excitement and vitality.

"Carlo," Alexis called over the rich sound that seemed to shimmer in the air. He cut off in mid-tone and whirled around to face her. There was a guilty look on his face, like that of an urchin caught yet again with his hand in the cookie jar.

"Carlo," she said again, softly. "Why didn't you tell me about having to sing in Rome? We could have worked harder and been finished by now."

"If I had told you, we would have worked harder, and now you would be going home rather than coming with me." He smiled ingenuously at her.

Sternly she reminded herself that she was *angry*. "Carlo, I have a business to run. I can't be away too long."

"But it is only nine days," he said coaxingly. "What is nine days in the life of a person?"

"God created the entire world in seven," she remarked with asperity.

"So it takes me a little longer." He chuckled.

"Longer for what?" she asked suspiciously.

He said nothing but allowed his eyes to devour the slender lines of her body. Alexis shivered, feeling as if his hand rather than his eyes had traced that sensual line. Suddenly he crossed to her, removed the travel books she clutched tightly to her breast, and captured her hands.

"Please, Alexis, please come with me."

His sincerity, and the warm touch of his hands, swept away all ability to resist him. She was once more overpowered, routed, defeated by him. She knew she should not accept, but she wanted to be with him, to be just a woman with a man she was fantastically attracted to rather than an efficient travel agent with her client.

Drawing a ragged breath, she gave a quick little nod. Carlo gave a great shout of joy and then leaned forward, capturing her lips with his. Each time before, his kisses had been quick, light caresses that left her longing for more. This kiss *was* more. His lips were soft yet insistent, as he played with and teased her sensitive mouth. She tried to press her lips together to resist the sensuous demands of his, but it was no use. With a sigh that was almost a moan, her lips parted, and their tongues met. Waves of faintness washed over her as his mouth possessed hers. Under the almost-suffocating demands of his lips and tongue, she felt the muscles in her thighs tighten and ache in response. Fire burned through Alexis' body, and, terrified by the intensity of her need, she pulled away from his embrace.

They stood only inches from each other, their breath coming in sharp gasps. The gold of Carlo's eyes was submerged in the dark passion smoldering there.

"We will not work today," he said softly. "I must pack and make plans, for you have told me something very important today."

Alexis did not pretend to misunderstand. In spite of her proud and brave words, both to Carlo and to herself, about her independence and capability, her lips had betrayed her.

Her need and her desire for Carlo had burned on her mouth. She ached to be held and captivated by him, to abandon her lonely stance as an embittered divorcée and career woman. Her cheeks were hot, and he touched them with his fingers, a welcome coolness against the inflamed skin.

"Go now," he ordered, stroking her cheek with the back of his hand. Alexis found herself obeying. She felt no urge to rebel at the command, as she would have done with Michael, or any other man but Carlo.

She had almost reached the door when he said casually, "I think I am winning the challenge."

She whirled to face him. "I'm not drunk yet," she stated, lifting her chin defiantly.

"You will be. Oh, yes, my darling, there is a wine we are going to share." His voice was husky with passion.

The terror and fascination of the hunted warred within her. Slowly, as if she had been mesmerized, she left the room.

And bumped soundly into Bianca, who gave a squeak of guilt.

"Bianca!" Alexis said accusingly. "Were you eavesdropping?"

"Yes, I mean no, I . . . I am a very poor liar," she amended with an engaging smile so like her brother's. "I am sorry, Alexis, but I had to know if you were to go with us."

"Why?" Alexis laughed. "Is the thought so horrifying?"

"In nessun modo," Bianca denied. "I was afraid you would decide to return to America, and I would not have an opportunity to really get to know you. But now you are to go, and it will be perfect. Please—come upstairs

and help me select some clothes. Truly, I have nothing to wear!"

"If *you* have nothing to wear, think how that makes *me* feel," Alexis protested, linking arms with the younger girl.

"Not to worry! We will put our heads together, you and I, and we will work miracles."

"I hope you're right. I was rather afraid our two heads might only equal one."

Bianca laughed and gave Alexis' arm an affectionate squeeze. "You are too hard on yourself, *amica mia*. As Carlo has said, you are a remarkable woman."

"Oh?" Alexis asked, drawing out the word slowly. "Just what else has Carlo said?"

"If I told you, then he couldn't," Bianca replied with an impudent grin. "And it is so much more effective if he tells you."

"If he bothers to. I'm beginning to feel a bit paranoid. Is everyone discussing me?"

Pausing, Bianca looked contritely at Alexis. "It's not what you think, Alexis. We talk, but there is no malice. How could there be?"

"Very easily," Alexis replied dryly. "I've been told I'm a very difficult and sulky person."

"By your ex-husband, no?"

"By my ex-husband, yes."

They had reached Bianca's room, and the Italian woman released Alexis' arm and pushed open the door. "If you would like, we could talk while I rummage. You did promise you would tell me about this husband," she reminded gently.

Alexis wondered if everything she said would go straight to Carlo. Suddenly she decided that wouldn't be so bad. After all, she had been really rude and ugly to Carlo several times during the past week, and if this was the only way to give him an explanation for her behavior, then so be it.

Having reached the decision, she smiled brightly at Bianca and said, "Sure, why not? Maybe I'll be able to exorcise my demon if I talk about him."

"I am a good Catholic, and so am, of course, versed in the matter of exorcism," Bianca responded with a straight face.

"All right, Mother Bianca, you asked for it. Prepare yourself for all the grim and gory details."

Alexis followed the Italian woman into the room, noting with approval the bright yellow-and-white color scheme. The room was more modern than others she had seen in the villa. The bed was simple without the over-powering canopy, and in place of the more classical art and sculpture which filled the house, there were impressionistic watercolors on the walls, and a large white porcelain cat sat serenely near the window.

Alexis assumed Bianca would want to pile her wardrobe onto the bed, so she opted to sit on a delicate brocaded lounge. As she sank onto it, she found she couldn't relax, and so perched nervously on the edge staring intently at her small feet. Now that she had agreed to do it, she wasn't at all sure she could open up. Only to her best friends and partners, François and Amy, had she revealed the nightmare that those three years with Michael had been. She hadn't even been able to turn to her father, who had been her mainstay for most of her life. In part she had been reluctant; she'd known he hadn't fully approved of her marriage, and she was afraid he would simply say he had told her so.

Bianca emerged from the huge walk-in closet, red-faced and panting under an enormous load of clothing. A steady rain of hangers followed her tottering progress to the bed.

"Why didn't you bring them out one at a time?" asked Alexis with a laugh.

"That would have been too logical. But now I am here, so begin."

Alexis allowed her mind to spin back to that first night when Michael had exploded into her life.

"My father was performing with the San Francisco Symphony," she said slowly. "I had gone backstage at intermission to see him, and to make sure he was all right. You see, the light on the piano had gone out halfway through the concerto, and little things like that can really throw a performer." Bianca nodded with understanding as she sorted swiftly through the pile of fabrics on the bed.

"Well, my dad is a quiet, shy man, and he was having a hard time attracting the attention of the stage crew. We were standing there looking helpless when this blond god stormed up to one of the stagehands and brandished his cello bow under the man's nose. He ordered the fellow onto the stage to repair the light, and then he joined us. Dad was grateful, and I must admit I was completely bowled over by his power, not to mention his looks."

"Good, eh?"

"The best," Alexis concurred, and for an instant she remembered him on their honeymoon in Sun Valley, his perfect body outlined under the wool of his alpine sweater and the tight ski pants, his hair silver-gold in the sunlight. "Anyway, we had coffee after the performance that night . . . and then we started dating. He was a very masterful man. Within days he had catalogued my faults, but he assured me the worst could be changed and the rest he was willing to overlook." Alexis looked up to meet Bianca's incredulous stare. "I know, I know. I feel like a real twit for putting up with it for a minute, but you don't know Michael." She paused and said softly, as though to herself, "I doubt anyone really knows Michael. He can convince anyone that black is white. When you're with him, he makes you feel that something exciting is about to happen. Later, though, I didn't want excitement. I wanted a normal family life."

"But you had no children."

"No. I discovered after we were married that Michael didn't want any. And what Michael wanted, Michael got."

"That must have been very hard for you."

"It was, but in some ways I'm glad for the way it worked out. Michael did such a thorough job of undermining me, I'd hate to see what he might have done to a child."

"Undermine? How do you mean, undermine?" Bianca frowned.

Alexis rose and walked quickly to the window. She gripped the drape and stared blindly out at the garden. She was so ashamed of her own weakness, and in spite of Bianca's kindness and affection, she was reluctant to reveal how Michael had enervated her and sapped her strength. Suddenly a gentle hand was slipped through hers, which hung limply at her side. She turned slowly to face Bianca, who gave her hand a brisk squeeze before releasing it.

"You don't have to ask anymore, Alexis. I did not realize when I asked about your marriage that this time was so painful for you. I think your husband must have been a great beast to have treated so fine and lovely a lady in such a fashion." Her gold-brown eyes sparkled with indignation.

Alexis smiled wanly at the other woman. "You're sweet to take my side so readily, Bianca, but in a lot of ways I asked for what happened to me. I never had much self-confidence anyway, and I think I married Michael so he could be strong and masterful for the two of us. I didn't have to worry—or so I thought. What I didn't stop to think about was that he would try to destroy what little self-confidence I did have. I made two really bad mistakes. One was trying to have someone live my life for me, and the other was staying once I realized what was happening."

She squared her shoulders and lifted her chin proudly.

"But all that is past now, and I'm finally becoming a real, live person who is able to stand on her own and doesn't need anyone to think for her."

Bianca returned to the bed, and smoothed the folds of a brown velvet skirt. In an almost too-casual tone she asked, "But don't you want to share your life with someone?"

"Of course, if it would be a sharing, and not a dominating, relationship. However, from my past experience—"

"You don't think such men exist, do you?" Bianca accused, interrupting Alexis, who blinked at her.

"That's not true. . . ." Alexis faltered to a halt, her innate honesty rebelling at the lie she was about to utter. She had begun to distrust all men. Particulary confident and powerful ones. *Men like Carlo Benoni,* one part of her whispered. But was it distrust that dictated her every response to the singer, or was it something else? Something like . . . Alexis wrenched her thoughts from that dangerous ground. Betrayed once today, she would not willingly walk into that trap again.

Hurrying to Bianca's side, she swept up a lovely maroon cocktail dress. "Here, we'd better start getting you organized, or you'll never get to Rome." Her words seemed brittle even to her own ears, and she ducked her head to avoid Bianca's curious look.

The morning passed swiftly and pleasantly. She helped Bianca hang up the rejects, then surveyed the mound of clothes that would go to Rome. Shaking her head, she gave a short laugh. "It looks like you're packing for a world cruise," she said.

"But Alexis," Bianca stated, "one *must* dress."

"One must also eat," came Ian's bright voice from the doorway. "Are you ladies going to join us, or are you going to spend the entire day in this boutique?"

"Lunch already!" Alexis exclaimed, checking her dainty wristwatch.

"Oh, no, are we late?" Bianca anxiously asked the small accompanist.

"Only to the extent that the soup has been cooling on the table for the past fifteen minutes, and your mother is in a fair taking."

Laughing guiltily, they raced down the stairs and into the dining room. Their heels clattered loudly on the hardwood floor, and Alexis had to grab the edge of the heavy table to stop her forward momentum.

Venezia was gazing morosely at her bowl of congealing cream-of-mushroom soup, and she gave Alexis and Bianca one deeply hurt and accusing look before lifting her spoon.

"Mama, forgive us," Bianca said, sliding into her seat. Gunther had leaped to assist her into her chair, and the expression in his eyes made Alexis wonder whether he was working for Carlo because of Carlo or for other, more personal reasons. For the first time she saw Gunther in a new light.

Alexis tried to move inconspicuously to her place, fearful that Carlo would rise to help her. She was shaken by the thought that he might touch her again. Every nerve in her body seemed charged and aware of him. She almost succeeded, but suddenly Carlo was there guiding her into the chair. As she sank onto the embroidered surface, he whispered, "I like that entrance. The way your feet sort of spun on the floor was marvelous. I know a hall that is even more highly polished, if you'd like to go floor skating with me." She gave him a withering look and shook out her napkin with a snap.

Carlo returned to his seat, and, folding his hands on the white lace tablecloth, he cleared his throat. Venezia paused, her spoon halfway to her mouth, and eyed her son suspiciously.

"I have an announcement to make."

"Ah, Carlo, no," wailed his mother. "Not at lunch. You are going to make everyone uncomfortable, I know, and spoil my digestion."

"Calmate, Mama," he soothed. "I think you will like this news." He paused and beamed at everyone. Ian and Bianca waited expectantly, while Gunther looked faintly bored. Alexis found herself alternately infuriated and amused by his sense of showmanship. For an instant their eyes met, and he winked, sending her into confusion.

"I have decided," he said at last, "to leave three days early and go first to Naples and Pompeii before we travel on to Rome."

"Carlo, that's wonderful!" Bianca tossed her napkin into the air with delight.

"Bene," Venezia added. "We can see the del Fiores. The last time I saw them was when we went to the Greek islands together. *She* has a new grandchild . . . her third. Unlike some women who have selfish and ungrateful children who will give them no grandchildren." She stared meaningfully at her son and daughter.

"We're working on it, Mama," Carlo assured her.

"And why was I not consulted about this trip?" The flat voice cut through the room, dampening the happy mood. Alexis glanced at the manager, noting the thin line of his lips and the angry color that spread across his cheeks.

Carlo continued to smile. Was he unaware of his manager's fury, or was he choosing to ignore it? she wondered.

"Now, Gunther," he began smoothly, "what difference does it make when we leave, so long as we are in Rome by Wednesday?"

"I planned your itinerary so that you would have sufficient time to prepare and rest before your performances. Sightseeing all over Naples and Pompeii is not what I had in mind."

His cold eyes flicked significantly to Alexis with his last sentence, and with a shiver she realized she had innocently deepened the hatred the manager felt for her.

"I am neither a child nor an invalid," Carlo retorted, his smile gone. "Besides, I want to show Alexis Naples by moonlight." His warm golden eyes caressed her, and Alexis felt as if she were once more enfolded in his embrace. Blushing, she stirred her soup, mentally cataloguing the number of mushrooms that floated languidly in the rich white broth. She willed herself not to look at him.

Gunther thrust back his chair and slapped his napkin onto the table. "As my decisions are being so cavalierly ignored, I must admit I wonder what I am being paid for. But then again, I am only a businessman. I lack the expertise of an American travel agent. Now, if you will excuse me . . ." The blond man strode to the door and exited without a backward glance.

Carlo half rose from his chair at Gunther's parting words, but Bianca's hand on his arm held him back. Above the beard his cheeks were suffused with red, and there was an angry glitter in his eyes. Bianca murmured softly to her brother in Italian for several moments, until, with a curt nod, he sank back into his chair. Venezia's shrewd eyes shot from Carlo to Alexis and then to the door. She gave a quick nod and turned her attention back to her meal. Ian, white-faced from the hostility, had shrunk back in his chair, his usually robust appetite gone.

Alexis knew something had to be done to end the now-overt hostility between Carlo and Gunther. Drawing in a deep breath, she set aside her spoon and shifted in her chair to face the singer.

"Carlo, I'm going to stay behind. There is absolutely no reason why I should go with you."

"No, please, I want you with me, and that is reason enough."

"Is it more important than your working relationship with Gunther?"

"Yes."

"Carlo, that's silly."

"You accepted as a friend to come with me. It would be rude and wrong of you to change your mind now." His eyes implored her. With a sigh she nodded, but she was not happy with her decision. She knew she didn't have full control of the situation, and she also knew with a frightening certainty that she was being brought ever closer to Carlo Benoni.

The next morning Alexis cautiously wove her way through the mounds of luggage adorning the front drive of the villa. Harried servants loaded the expensive leather cases into the trunks of two waiting cars, while Venezia added to the confusion by issuing contradictory and usually incomprehensible instructions.

Ian, toting an enormous picnic basket, gently took Venezia's arm and removed her from the top step of the entryway. She fell upon the small man with cries of joy and allowed him to escort her to her car. Moments later, Bianca bustled from the villa, pulling on her gloves and giving her pretty hat one final pat so that it rested at an even jauntier angle.

Alexis felt lost and very out of place in the midst of all the activity. Her designer jeans and velour top had seemed appropriate for a long drive, until she'd seen Bianca in her linen suit, gloves, and hat. She shifted her single case to her other hand and wished, not for the first time, that she were home. Why did everything seem right at home and wrong here?

"Eh! Alexis! Are you going to stand there all morning? I intend to be waiting for these slowpokes in Naples." She gazed down the long drive and saw Carlo leaning against the hood of a very long, very sleek, very red Ferrari.

"Do you expect me to ride in *that?*"

"But of course. It only seats two, and you are the only two I want."

"That doesn't make any sense," she remarked acidly, even as her feet carried her down the white gravel drive to his side.

He reached down and took the case, their hands brushing. Alexis' stomach knotted from the brief contact, and she wondered how she would ever survive the drive, locked in such close quarters with Benoni.

"This is all you have?" Carlo queried as he placed the single case into the trunk.

"Uh huh. How much does one woman need?"

"Could we run back and have you repeat that to my mother and sister?" Taking her elbow, he walked her to the passenger side of the car and helped her squeeze in. "You know something?" he added, leaning on the door. "I think I'm going to marry you. A woman who can travel light would be a great advantage to a performer like myself."

"I thought you'd leave her at home with the babies so you could flirt with your adoring fans," she quipped, even as she tried to still the uncomfortable way her heart was racing.

Carlo smiled raffishly and slammed the door. As he slid into the driver's seat and started the engine, he casually asked, "You like babies?"

Alexis, who had once again been wondering how she had gotten into this mess, was startled by the sudden question, and answered honestly and without thinking. "Yes, of course." A slow smile crossed Carlo's round face, and she mentally kicked herself for encouraging him, no matter how innocently.

Carlo released the brake and put the car in gear, and they raced away from the villa. As they roared down the hill, he cast a sidelong glance at Alexis and grinned happily.

"On to Naples and the moonlight," he called over the rush of air through the open windows. "And the Cave of the Sibyl."

"What's that?" Alexis yelled, clutching vainly at her wildly blowing hair.

"The home of the sibyl, a wise woman who could foretell the future. She guided Aeneas to the Underworld so he could found Rome. I only hope I will not need to go to such lengths to fulfill my dream."

She suspected Carlo's dream was of a warm and secure home life, with a wife and children, but did he mean to make her the mistress of that home? Somehow she thought not. She suspected he would like to enjoy a brief and passionate affair, and though she desired him in all senses of the word, she wasn't willing to settle for the dubious honor of being Carlo's mistress. To think of more was simply inconceivable. She conjured an image of the bright poster-bedecked walls of World Seekers, and told herself that there was more to life than Carlo Benoni.

CHAPTER
Seven

"AH, MY LITTLE *pulcino,*" Carlo said sympathetically as he opened the door of the car, "you are as white as marble."

"Who wouldn't be after that drive?" Alexis responded somewhat feebly. "Carlo, you're a maniac!"

"A glass of wine and a hot bath, and you will feel more the thing."

"That sounds lovely, but it is *not* going to change my opinion of you and your driving."

Chuckling, Carlo cupped her chin in his hand. "You need some danger in your life. You think you want to be safe and secure, but underneath I feel the excitement in you. You try to make everyone think you are the so-capable and professional American business lady, but in reality you are just like that mountain." He gestured to the lowering presence of Vesuvius. "It is quiet now, but a thin wisp of smoke curling over its peak is like a promise of fire and passion." Alexis felt her mouth go dry and swallowed convulsively several times.

"How about the wine?" she at last managed to say.

"I think I'm beginning to make progress," Carlo remarked as they followed the porter into the hotel. "A week ago you would have taken the bath first."

Alexis gave him a speaking look and stepped ahead of him. Behind her she could hear his merry laughter, and she fought the impulse to laugh with him.

Carlo sent the porter up to their rooms with the bags and then led her into the elegant bar of the hotel. Chandeliers of red crystal cast a subdued light over the wood-paneled room. There were few people in the bar at this time of day, and a brace of waiters rushed to serve them. They were given a small table tucked intimately away in a corner. Carlo exchanged a rapid-fire burst of Italian with the waiter who reached them first, and then settled back comfortably in his chair to stare appreciatively at Alexis.

Glancing about the expensively furnished room, Alexis felt a definite cramp in her pocketbook. Taking a deep breath, she met Carlo's eyes and began.

"I will, of course, be paying for my expenses during this trip," she said firmly.

"Nonsense. This is part of your work."

"Now, that really *is* nonsense, Carlo. This is simply an interruption, albeit a pleasant one, in our work."

"No, no," he disagreed, his face expressionless. "This is research."

"What?"

"Yes. You see, you are learning my habits so you can better plan for me."

"That is the most ridiculous thing I've ever heard."

The waiter had returned, and with a flourish set delicate crystal glasses before them.

"This is Lacrimedi Cristo, or 'Tears of Christ,'" Carlo explained, once more deftly changing the topic. "The grapes are grown on the slopes of Vesuvius. I'm interested to see what effect it will have on you."

Alexis' face burned at his reference, but she met his laughing eyes. Picking up her glass, she gazed at him over the rim, saying sweetly, "It will probably just increase my already irascible temper, and I'll explode like that volcano, the next time you try to boss me around."

He touched his chest, giving her a "who, me?" look that made her laugh.

She savored that tart dryness of the white wine and nodded her approval.

"Do you feel anything?" Carlo asked hopefully.

"Uh huh." He leaned forward expectantly. "Tired."

"American!" he said disgustedly, falling back in his chair.

"Italian!" she mimicked in the same tone. "But back to the expenses of this trip. . . Will you at least let me buy you dinner?"

"No, never. A gentleman would never treat a lady so."

"But you're not a gentleman," she responded, her eyes twinkling.

"Brat," he grumbled. "Okay, so I am still practicing. Why don't you go rest? Maybe it just takes a little time for the wine to work," he added, glancing at her empty glass.

"We'll test out your theory at dinner."

"How about after dinner?"

"*At* dinner," she repeated firmly. Blowing him a kiss, she hurried from the bar.

* * *

Early the next morning Alexis bounced down the stairs to the lobby, swinging her straw hat by its green ribbons. Over dinner, the now-reunited party had discussed plans for the next three days. In between bites of shrimp scampi they had decided to spend a full day going to Capri and the Blue Grotto, leaving Naples and Pompeii for the remaining two days.

Alexis paused before an oval, gilt-edged mirror in the lobby and surveyed her reflection. She wore a thin green linen dress and sandals, for it was much warmer here than in Florence. Her ebony hair fell smoothly to her shoulders, caressing her cheek and neck as she tossed her head. She smiled, feeling suddenly so *good* for the first time in many months.

She hurried into the restaurant, to find Bianca and Venezia already rising from the table. The fact that Venezia was up so early was startling enough, but the two Italian women's outfits were what stopped Alexis in mid-stride. From the top of their dainty lace-and-velvet hats to the tips of their gloved fingers, they were the picture of chic and sophistication. It was obvious they weren't planning to come on any boat ride.

"Bianca, what, I mean . . . well, where are you going?" she finished lamely.

"Oh, dearest Alexis, please say you will forgive us, but our old friends the del Fiores called us last night and insisted we come to visit. I hope you won't mind, but I know you and Carlo will enjoy Capri."

The explanation was delivered in the sincerest of tones, but Alexis was certain a gleam lurked deep in Bianca's gold-brown eyes.

"But what about Ian?" Alexis asked, grabbing at her last straw. "He was coming with us."

"Ah, the *poverino,*" sighed Venezia. "He is not feeling well today. Too much garlic in the scampi, I think." She tried to look mournful but only succeeded in looking like a cat faced with a dish of cream.

"Bianca, you rat," Alexis murmured in an undertone to the younger girl. "I'll get you for this."

"Shhhh, Carlo is coming, and you don't want him to think you are threatening me, do you? *Addio,* darlings," she called brightly to Carlo and Alexis. "Have fun." With a jaunty wave, she linked arms with her mother, and they swept from the restaurant.

"You would like some breakfast?" Carlo asked affably.

"No, what I'd really like to do is chew nails. You're behind this," Alexis accused.

"But of course not," he said smoothly, stroking his beard. Amusement gleamed in his extraordinary eyes. "I'm much too simple and honest a person to be part of such an act of duplicity."

"I'll bet," muttered Alexis, but she allowed Carlo to escort her to the table and pull out a chair for her.

She crumbled a flaky croissant between her fingers and tried to see a way out of spending the entire day alone with him. Solution presented itself immediately, and she had to admit she really did want to see the lovely island that had been the playground for Roman emperors and was now the retreat for the wealthy the world over. She decided to ignore the trick that had been played on her and enjoy the outing anyway.

Carlo mopped up the last bite of his eggs and grabbed several rolls from the basket next to his elbow, stuffing them into his pocket.

Seeing her scandalized expression, he shrugged contritely. "What if we are shipwrecked?" he asked plaintively.

"In the middle of a bay? Carlo, really."

"Well, I can hope. We would be washed ashore on a tiny Mediterranean island. Your clothes would, of course, be soaked and torn from the wreck, so I would build a shelter and a fire and take you in my arms to warm you—"

"That's quite enough of that, and by the way, when was the last time I told you you were totally impossible? Now, let's go!"

Alexis grasped his arm firmly with both hands and pulled him from the hotel.

Carlo had decided they would take the steamer from Vico Equense rather than Naples, so Alexis could see some of the famed Amalfi Drive. Parking the car at the dock, they purchased tickets and boarded the small boat. The salty tang of the air made Alexis think suddenly of home, but strangely she found she felt no homesickness. Before she had a chance to ponder this further, Carlo's arm slid warmly about her waist, and he rested his cheek against hers.

"There to our right is Naples, and you can really get a view of Vesuvius from here. A few kilometers south of here is Sorrento, which is perhaps the most beautiful town in Italy. Alas, we have no time to see it this trip, but there will always be a next time."

The surety with which he stated that they would be together again left Alexis filled with happiness, but realistically she knew there was little chance of her returning to Italy anytime soon. Still, it gave her a warm glow to know Carlo obviously wanted her to come back.

Much too soon, the tiny mountain island loomed before them, and the steamer slid easily to the dock at Marina Grande.

"I have hired a taxi for the day," Carlo said as they stepped ashore. "He will take us first to the grotto so we can see it when the light is perfect. Then we will go to Anacapri, which is the upper town, for lunch at the Caesar Augustus Café, where you will have a true pizza."

"It sounds delightful."

"With you as my companion, it will be," Carlo whispered against her ear. His warm breath caressed the sensitive skin of her lobe, and liquid fire raced down her spine.

Alexis suddenly pulled off her hat, allowing the breeze to lift her heavy hair. Then, smiling, she offered Carlo her hand. Hand in hand, they ran to the small, battered blue Fiat, where a bronzed young man, his white shirt open to reveal his chest, waited, watching them with amusement.

"Taddeo?" Carlo asked, panting.

"Si."

"I am Signor Benoni, and this is Signorina Alexis."

The young man nodded politely to Carlo and frankly appraised Alexis' trim figure, well outlined beneath the thin material of her dress.

Carlo pulled open the back door, then paused before climbing in after Alexis. "Eh, Taddeo."

"Si, signore?"

"You can look and admire, but don't touch."

"Carlo." Alexis giggled.

"Believe me, I know what I'm doing. These Italian men are all the same."

This was uttered in so pious a tone that Alexis gave up and began to laugh.

"You think I'm joking? But see." He swooped down, kissing her firmly on the lips. "None of us can be trusted."

"You've told me that before," Alexis replied, but this time she was not filled with hurt at his remark. She had learned to know the big Italian enough to recognize a joke when she heard one. And, she added to herself, she had grown enough to be able to take a joke.

They began the drive to the famed Blue Grotto. As she gazed at the soaring peaks dotted with unknown ruins, Alexis felt a touch of mysterious evil.

Turning to face her companion, she found Carlo studying her. She smiled in response and said, "Looking at all this, I have to admit I feel like I've stepped back into a Greek myth."

Carlo smiled, revealing even white teeth between his dark beard and mustache. "Ah, but, my Alexis, you have. This is a magical place." He slipped an arm about her shoulders and leaned forward, his cheek brushing against hers, and pointed out the open window. "Look, look up there."

She followed the direction of his pointing finger and gazed at the jewellike grotto ringed with stones.

"Can't you see the nymphs and satyrs dancing there?"

She stole a glance at his darkly bearded face, with its firm and mobile lips, and wondered if maybe one of those mythological creatures hadn't escaped from these mountains to join her in the small car.

The road took a sudden curve and brought them to the edge of the island overlooking the bay.

"From here we take a rowboat into the grotto proper," Carlo explained. They had soon rented one of the small crafts from an ancient man who seemed more a part of the rocky cliffs than a living person. Seated comfortably side by side, they watched as the old man sculled swiftly toward the limestone cliffs.

The mouth of a cavern yawned before them, and then they were inside. Alexis gasped. It was if she had entered into the heart of a sapphire.

"It is lovely, no?"

"Oh, Carlo, it is lovely, yes," she breathed. He was very close to her in the azure confines of the grotto. She could feel the warmth and energy radiating from him, and she longed to melt against him, to feel his powerful arms around her once more.

"What . . . what caused the color?" she asked, trying to mask her confusion and desire.

"The refraction of the light through the water and onto the walls."

"That's beyond me."

"Me also, but now, if you have seen enough, I am hungry—"

"Why don't you eat your rolls?" she suggested sweetly.

"Hush!" he ordered, and kissed her on the nose. "And also I do not wish to be trapped in here when the tide comes in."

"That I agree with," said Alexis, glancing nervously about the suddenly ominous cavern. "Let's go."

They were soon in Anacapri, a tiny town of twisting streets and stucco buildings. At the Caesar Augustus Café, they were seated outdoors, overlooking the beautiful island panorama. There was, of course, wine to accompany the hot slices of pizza thick with cheese, vegetables, and topped with anchovies.

"Carlo," said Alexis, pushing aside her plate, "I wanted to ask you something."

"Si?" He patted at his lips with a large white napkin and waited expectantly.

"I don't know what it is, but as beautiful as this island is, I still have a feeling of . . . well, an ancient evil. Does that make any sense?"

"Oh, yes. You are sensing an echo of the Emperor Tiberius and the orgies which took place at his villa."

"I always thought he was in exile here." Alexis frowned.

"Well, in a sense, but it was a self-imposed exile. Here, far from the prying eyes of Rome, he could indulge in the kind of debauchery he liked best. But the rumors got back to the capital, and the tales of his cruelty and sadism turned the people against him."

"You talk about satyrs," said Alexis. "It sounds to me as if the real people were wild enough, without bringing in mythical ones."

"True. Still, it is interesting how much of Roman history turns on the oddities of the emperors. Caligula began his reign blessed with great popularity, but at the end he was killed by his own guard, who had become utterly disgusted with his obscene, mad rule."

Leaning back in her chair, Alexis watched with pleasure the emotions that flitted across Carlo's handsome face as he talked of the history of his country. Again she was struck by the depth of his knowledge and the breadth of his interests.

Being the child of an instrumentalist, and the wife of one, however briefly, she had an instrumentalist's disdain for singers. She had heard all her life that singers were stupid people. But in Carlo's company she'd begun to reject this childhood implanting. Carlo's knowledge of history and politics was encyclopedic, and, more importantly, thoughtful and incisive. He was not a person who dully repeated facts memorized in school, but a man of great intelligence.

Draining the last of his wine, he winked at her. "I think we had better go, or we will end up spending the night here, and I do not wish to ruin your reputation."

"Is that ever a fib!" exclaimed Alexis.

He grinned wolfishly. "I am trying to lull you. That is the first rule when besieging someone."

But as she took his arm, she thought she was still not ready or able to love Carlo.

Her long black velvet skirt whispered across the carpet in her hotel room as Alexis snapped off the small lamp by her bed and crossed to the balcony, pushing open the windows. As she gazed out over the bay, the city lay in a glittering arc about the dark waters, and the light on the moored ships bodded gently with the motion of the waves. She knew she should be tired from the two days of frantic sightseeing, but instead she felt a heady excitement filling her veins.

The day after their outing to Capri, she and Carlo had rambled through Naples, visiting the National Museum, the Castel Nuovo, the Capodimonte gallery. She hadn't even objected when Bianca had pleaded a headache, and Venezia had saved herself the exertion of lying, by simply not appearing. Once more she had found herself alone with the handsome singer.

With a sigh she rested her elbows on the railing and thought drowsily about her day—the ice cream they had shared in the piazza, the religious festival they had stumbled into, and the laughter, always the laughter. They had even managed to dine alone, where they talked of their childhoods. But not of the future, for Alexis was so confused that the future seemed a murky void.

Suddenly she jerked upright, as she realized that for two full days she hadn't been tortured with errant memories of Michael. She wrapped her arms ecstatically about herself and called out across the silent water.

"You know, little ghost, you're becoming very pale."

A soft knock on the door brought her flying back into the room. She pulled open the door and found Carlo whistling merrily as he waited.

"Carlo, what are you doing here? It must be near eleven."

"Later, but not to worry. We have one more place to visit."

"Carlo, you're crazy," she said, but offered no resistance when he wrapped her shawl about her and hurried her down the stairs and out of the hotel.

He drove without speaking, but the silence was very companionable, particularly since Carlo kept Alexis' hand in his the entire way.

"This is the Certosa di San Martino," Carlo said at last as they pulled up to the darkened building. "They are closed until morning, but I know they will not mind our using their balcony. From there one can have the finest view of Naples and the bay. And look, the moon is rising."

On the side of the building were shallow steps leading

up to the broad balcony. As they hurried up to the gallery, Alexis gave a tiny laugh. "We'll probably be arrested."

"They will know that we are lovers, and, being good Italians, the officers will leave us be." His gold-brown gaze dared her to disagree.

She lifted her chin proudly and stared him down. He sighed, sounding a bit defeated, and said, "Okay, we will just tell them we are crazy. And that I am *trying* to be your lover."

"That's better."

They reached the balcony and stood hand in hand, gazing out over the incomparable view of the city and bay. The moon rode serenely over all, turning the waters of the bay to molten silver.

For a long time they remained in silence, wrapped in secret thoughts and sharing their closeness. Alexis realized that for the first time in years she was at peace. The emotion was so new that she spent a long moment savoring it, then with a tiny sigh of happiness she looked up at Carlo.

"Thank you," she whispered.

"You are welcome," he murmured.

"But you don't know what I was going to say."

"Oh, yes, I do, for I know your heart, my darling."

He lifted her hair, its silken darkness spilling over his hands. His thumbs began to caress her high cheekbones. She raised her head, his warm breath fluttering on her face; her lips parted softly in anticipation of the kiss.

Slowly and with infinite gentleness he bent, his lips touching hers with the passion and quietness of the volcano he had likened her to. For the first time since their tempestuous meeting Alexis was open and ready for the embrace that now captured her. With a moan her lips parted, welcoming the sweet probings of his tongue. Carlo explored her mouth with practiced ease, and shivering waves of pleasure washed through her body, leaving her knees weak.

Suddenly his mouth became more demanding, and his hands began an almost harsh stroking, pulling her tightly against his chest and thighs. Not releasing her mouth, he slipped one hand into the inviting vee of her lace blouse, probing, seeking the soft curve of her bosom. A roaring filled her ears, and her blood hammered in her temples, beating out a primitive desire that swept in ever-rising waves through her body. Carlo's fingers plucked with feverish urgency at the buttons of her delicate blouse, seeking to free her breasts.

Alexis felt fear rising through the ache of her desire. She opened her eyes and pressed one hand against his chest, trying to push him away. He gave a growl of displeasure and pulled her closer.

"Carlo," she panted, twisting her mouth away from his. "Please . . . stop. I don't know . . . I'm not sure."

He stepped back, frustration etched in his body. "How much longer?" he demanded. "How much longer must I wait? I am a patient man, Alexis, but . . ." He shrugged furiously and walked away to lean heavily on the stone balustrade.

Alexis backed against the rough stone of the monastery and pressed her hands to her temples. She wanted him but she couldn't trust him, and the contradiction was tearing her to pieces. The moonlight seemed suddenly icy, and she shivered in the lonely wind.

CHAPTER *Eight*

"YOU DON'T LIKE it here, do you?" Alexis asked.

They stood in the temple of Apollo while the wind whispered mournfully through the ruins, and the ghosts of Pompeii whispered with it.

Carlo turned slowly from his contemplation of the stark pillars and the lonely god who stood patiently waiting for the worshipers who never came. Silently he shook his head.

"Then why did we come here?" Alexis asked softly.

"I knew you would want to see it. I listened to the way you talked of Rome, over dinner the other night, and I thought to myself, Carlo, this is a lady who will understand Pompeii." He tried to force a gay lilt into his voice, but it fell flat and dull in the empty ruins.

"But you love all the glory that was Rome. So why are you so disturbed here?"

He shrugged helplessly and paced away, the dust rising with each step. "They were all living happily with their wives and their children . . ."

"Yes?" Alexis encouraged.

He drew a deep breath, filling his barrel chest. With a gust of air he released it, shaking his head. "And then, in a short afternoon, they were gone, dead, and now not even history mourns them."

Alexis cocked her head to one side, puzzled by this side of the man, which she had never seen. Carlo had always seemed so gay and carefree. Shallow, Michael would have called him. Yet here he was hurting over the destruction of a city almost two thousand years ago.

Adjusting her handbag more securely on her shoulder, she walked quietly up behind him and tentatively touched his arm. He wrapped his arms about her waist and rested his chin on the top of her dark head.

"You were sweet to bring me here, but I've seen enough. Let's go now, shall we?"

"You are sure? I don't want my foolishness to spoil your day."

She placed a forefinger over his lips. "Shhhh. You have to get to Rome today, and we don't want the others to arrive too many hours before we do. Although, the way you drive, we may beat them there yet."

"Devil," he growled. "The way I drive indeed. I am a magnificent driver."

"You'd have to be to have lived this long," Alexis retorted dryly.

They walked back through the cobbled streets of Pompeii, past small groups of tourists, who wandered awestruck through the shops of the artisans and the villas of the wealthy, now long-dead residents of the city. Carlo began to chuckle as he watched a red-faced tourist brusquely refuse to tip the guard who had unlocked one of the many gates of Pompeii.

"What's so funny?"

"Some of the famous pornography of Pompeii lies behind that gate, but I'm afraid that gentleman is going to have more time to appreciate it than he would like."

"How so?"

"He didn't tip the guard for opening the gate, and now the fellow will no doubt lock him in and forget about him."

"That's terrible," exclaimed Alexis, but she couldn't keep from laughing.

"At least this man will learn a valuable lesson. . . ."

"When in Rome," Alexis chimed in with Carlo as they located the bright-red sportscar.

"You didn't offer to show me any of the famous pornography of Pompeii," Alexis remarked as they pulled onto the highway.

"I didn't want you looking at it. I was afraid it might dilute your enthusiasm for practicing a little."

"I never practice pornography," she responded smartly. "It's something you have to fall into on the spur of the moment, as it were. But tell me, was your father a musician too?" Alexis asked, turning the topic toward a safer area.

"Lord, no." Carlo laughed, shaking his head at the thought. "No, he was a banker."

"A banker?" Alexis echoed, stunned. "But didn't he want you to be a banker like him?"

"Oh no, *cara,* you must understand the Italian mind. If you can't have a priest in the family, at least try for a singer."

"Well, that he certainly got."

"You realize, Alexis, that this will be the first time you have ever really heard me sing in performance."

"I'm looking forward to it. Four days until the opera opens, right?"

"Si, but it occurs to me that maybe I should treat you to the joys of my voice before that."

"In what way?" Alexis asked suspiciously, not liking the way the corners of Carlo's eyes were crinkling.

"I think maybe I'll come with a small troupe and serenade you beneath your hotel window. And then you would lean seductively over the balcony, your robe falling softly open to reveal the pure expanse of your bosom, and then you would throw me a single rose—"

"Chamber pot."

"Rose," he continued firmly. "And I would snatch the tender blossom from the air and press fervent kisses onto its fragrant petals." Carlo took both hands from the wheel and, catching the invisible flower, kissed it ecstatically, all the while watching Alexis. With a squawk Alexis grabbed for the wheel.

The car swerved, and Carlo quickly caught the wheel and righted it.

"For that stunt you'll get not only the chamber pot, but the day's garbage as well," Alexis scolded.

"You are too harsh," he complained, gazing at her with sad eyes.

"And you are too silly."

"Si."

"Buon giorno," Alexis said somewhat self-consciously as she joined Carlo and Bianca at breakfast the day after their arrival in Rome.

"Buon giorno, darling." Carlo patted his lips with the napkin and tossed it aside. "And *addio."*

"Addio?"

"I am due at rehearsal." He glanced at his watch. "Now. Have fun, my dears. I will see you sometime."

Alexis sank slowly into a chair and watched as Carlo

made his way through the closely-spaced tables. She suddenly became aware of numerous female eyes which followed the singer with longing and inviting looks, and a stab of jealously shot through her.

"It is not easy, is it?" Bianca said sympathetically.

Mutely Alexis shook her head.

"It is going to be bad for the next four days, until the opera opens," Carlo's sister said. "Rehearse, rehearse, rehearse, and when he is around he is always cranky."

"Why?" asked Alexis, seizing upon this new bit of information about Benoni.

"Because he hates to work hard, and when he is preparing for a role he must *work*. But anyway, for now we must do without him."

"That's fine," Alexis said, feigning an indifference she didn't feel. "In some ways your brother is much too exhausting. A rest will do me good."

"I hope you don't mean to truly rest. I was going to show you Rome and do some shopping."

"Don't worry." Alexis laughed. "I don't intend to take to my bed. I just thought a breather from Carlo would do me good."

"Bene! Now, where would you like to go today?"

"I'll let you be the tour guide. I think I've forgotten how, during the past three days."

"All right, then, I think we'll do this chronologically. Ancient Rome first, and then forward."

"Sounds great."

"This is going to be fun," the younger girl agreed happily.

"Just let me drink this coffee and put on my walking shoes, and I'll be ready."

They were chatting on the steps of the hotel, waiting for their taxi, when a cold and all-too-familiar voice snapped, "What? Not hard at work, Miss Dimitroff?"

Alexis flushed with anger and guilt, for she knew her

presence in Naples and Rome had little to do with her true purpose for being in Italy.

Seeing her distress, Bianca placed an affectionate hand on Alexis' arm. "Now, Gunther," she admonished, "don't be pedantic. Alexis is here as our guest, and a very welcome one she is, too."

Alexis lifted her eyes to meet Gunther's stony gaze. With a tremor of dread she realized he wasn't going to let it go at that. There was a set to his square jaw that indicated he was ready for a fight. Alexis had been raised in an atmosphere of quiet consideration. She had rarely seen her father angry, so she had been ill-prepared for Michael's tight-lipped fury. After enduring it for almost three years she found she could not cope with unpleasantness.

"Do you realize, Miss Dimitroff, just what your services to date have cost Signor Benoni?" the manager asked coldly. "I took the liberty of totaling the cost of your presence on this jaunt, and you're a very expensive proposition. I just hope Carlo has found you worth the—"

The insinuation was clear. Sickened, Alexis turned away, praying she could somehow miraculously be carried back home to San Francisco. Suddenly she heard the resounding smack of a hand on skin, and Bianca said shrilly, "You will never speak to a friend of mine in such a fashion again! You may be assured that my brother will hear of this—"

"Bianca, please, no," Alexis moaned faintly, horrified at the scene she had inadvertently caused.

"You work for my brother; you do not own him," Bianca continued heedlessly, ignoring Alexis' murmured protests. An interested crowd had begun to gather, and Alexis, now completely mortified, fled back into the safety of the hotel.

Rushing past goggling porters and patrons, she

reached the haven of her room. Shutting the door, she rested her back against its comforting firmness and allowed the tears to come.

She sobbed bitterly for several minutes, the hot tears scalding her as much as the knowledge that Gunther was right. She had behaved in a very unprofessional manner. She had allowed herself to take advantage of a client. Hesitantly she circled the room, looking through tear-dimmed eyes at the lovely furnishings. Bleakly she wondered just how much Carlo *had* spent.

Pulling open her handbag, she located a tissue and gave her nose a defiant blow. There was no more time for tears. She needed to go to the opera house, locate Carlo, and pay him for her accommodations over the past four days. She would then book herself into a less-expensive hotel and spend the next few days putting the finishing touches on Carlo's itinerary. She felt she now knew him well enough to make decisions without his being present. Besides, she reassured herself, he could always okay her choices later.

Bianca was in the elevator when Alexis entered it. The Italian woman eyed her suspiciously and asked, "Where are you going?"

"Out."

"Oh, no, you don't. You are not going to the opera."

"And what makes you think I am?"

"Your face is an open book," the younger girl responded bluntly, as the elevator reached the lobby. "Now, come here and sit down." Keeping a firm grip on Alexis' elbow, she propelled the other woman to a couch secluded in a corner.

"Sit down and listen! If you go to the opera, you will interrupt the rehearsal. On top of that, you will upset Carlo, who will leave the rehearsal and come looking for me so that he can find out what has happened. This will infuriate Maestro Salvatori, and he will fire Carlo, for he is that type of fellow, and then Carlo will fire Gunther, which may not be such a bad thing, but I submit to you that this is not the time or the place for such a thing. Now do you see why you must not go to the opera?"

"Yes, but Bianca, I have to repay Carlo," Alexis cried miserably.

"Fine; you may take that up with Carlo when we are back in Florence. But what you have to do this instant is accompany me to the Forum. I like you very much, Alexis, and I want to be your friend. Please let me."

The sincerity in the other woman's voice cut through Alexis' misery, and she discovered that she really did want to be a friend to Bianca—and not just because she was Carlo's sister, but because she was Bianca.

She smiled timorously at the lovely Italian and gave a tiny laugh. "You know, you and your brother are both immovable objects. I would love to see the Forum, and I can't think of anyone I'd rather see it with."

"Except Carlo," Bianca teased with a wicked smile.

Alexis gathered the shreds of her dignity about her and responded loftily, "Bianca, sometime I'm going to make you realize your brother is merely a friend and a client."

"Someday pigs will fly," Bianca said with a snort.

Alexis hugged the dress box with all the joy of a greedy child on Christmas morning. After exhausting the sights of Rome, she and Bianca had turned their attention to the boutiques the city had to offer, and that afternoon Alexis had found a dress she could not resist. Kicking shut the door of the hotel room, she hurried to the bed and deposited the box on the dark-blue bedspread. She gazed longingly at the long white carton elegantly tied with silver and gold ribbons and wondered if it was foolish to want to put on the dress again.

The desire was too strong to resist, and she swiftly

slipped off the simple jumper she had worn on the shopping expedition. Finally the last ribbon fell away from the box, and she was able to lift the lovely gown from its bed of tissue.

The black satin shimmered as she held the dress up to the light. Instead of her usual high-necked, well-covered style, this gown plunged daringly in the front and back, revealing the creamy sweep of her chest and back.

She pulled the dress on, reveling in the cool caress of the satin. Approaching a mirror, she bundled her hair haphazardly onto her head and studied the effect. Well, there was no doubt she wasn't as beautiful as the probably countless other women Carlo Benoni knew, but secretly she hoped that when she wore this to the opera tomorrow night it would drive the image of those other women from his mind.

The past four days had been a lesson in frustration. Bianca had been a charming companion, and Rome had proved to be truly the eternal city. Yet even in her enjoyment there had been a small hollow within her that not even Bianca's friendly presence could fill.

She missed Carlo Benoni.

There. It was finally out. She had admitted it. She had been the center of his attention in Naples, and she had hoped Rome would be the same. Instead she had seen him three times in the past four days, and each time he had been tired and preoccupied.

Before they had left on this trip, Carlo had said she would be the right kind of wife for a singer, but was that true? In Florence he had been mobbed by adoring women fans, and the jealousy that had seized her had eaten at her like acid. Also it was obvious that after his American tour he would be even more of a public figure than he already was. Then there was Rome. He was preparing for a role, and so he was never with her, but rather always at rehearsals. She needed something more homelike and stable. Living as a wife to a superstar was simply beyond her. She shook her head, deciding she couldn't take it.

"Good heavens!" she exclaimed, hitting her forehead lightly with a clenched fist. "What are you thinking of!" He hadn't even mentioned marriage.

Agitated, she paced about the hotel room. A scant few weeks ago she had been busily bragging about how independent she was and how she didn't need some man to be bossing her around. And now, dear God, here she was mooning over a man she had known for only two weeks, and thinking about marriage!

She raced to the bed and pulled off the black dress. Hastily she folded it, and started to replace it in the ivory box. Tomorrow, she decided, she would return it to the store.

She hesitated, the folds of material clutched desperately in both hands, and sank forlornly onto the bed. She should return the dress, she knew, yet she did so want to wear it tomorrow night when the opera opened.

But did she want the gown for her own pleasure? Or was she doing what she had vowed she would never do again—dressing for a man?

"I bought the dress because it was beautiful, and because it is the kind of thing Michael would never have permitted me to wear . . ." Her voice, so strong and sure at the beginning of her speech, whispered into silence.

The empty box mocked her, daring her to replace the dress and close the lid. *Oh, no!* she cried inwardly. *Are you falling in love with Carlo Benoni?*

CHAPTER *Nine*

ALEXIS RESTED A gloved hand on the velvet-covered railing of the Benoni box at the Rome Opera House and leaned forward to better appreciate the beauty of the old building. The tiers of seats curved away in both directions from where she sat, in the second-level center. The gold, crimson, and crystal decor of the interior dazzled the eye, as did the glittering assemblage who had gathered for this opening night of *A Masked Ball*. A confused clamor rose from the pit as individual instrumentalists in the orchestra ran quickly over difficult musical passages from the opera.

The door to the box was still open, as Bianca and Venezia were busy chatting with friends in the hall.

Bianca had been introducing Alexis to everyone in Rome, it seemed, but at last Alexis had ducked into the box to be alone. Somewhere behind the enormous red curtain Carlo waited. She wondered if he was thinking of her, or if all of his attention was directed toward the demanding role he must perform. She knew it was silly of her, but she hoped he had spared a thought for her. She shivered slightly, remembering the last time his lips had brushed hers.

Smiling, she cocked her head to allow the velvet touch of the orchid corsage to caress her cheek. The messenger from the florist had arrived as she was dressing. Inside the cream-colored carton had rested the spray of amber-tinted orchids. Beneath them was a card written in Carlo's elegant, flowing script. Now Alexis peeked quickly over her shoulder to be sure she was still unobserved, and hurriedly pulled the silver-embossed card from her small handbag.

Tesoro mio. Tonight is special because you will be there.

A simple and short note, but it made up for the loneliness of the past four days. It had, however, done nothing to calm the confusion that raged within her. The basic question remained; what did she feel for Carlo Benoni?

A single, pure tone rose from the orchestra pit. It was the concertmaster playing an "A" so that the orchestra could tune up. These preparations brought Bianca and Venezia hurrying into the box.

"Where's Ian?" Alexis asked as Bianca settled with a rustle of rose chiffon onto the chair next to hers.

"Making sure Gunther won't be joining us."

"Oh, Bianca, I never wanted to be such a source of dissension in your house!" Alexis tugged agitatedly at the tops of her gloves and gazed out, unseeing, at the audience on the lower level.

"It is not you, Alexis. This trouble began months ago

when Carlo decided to go to America, but Gunther is a coward, so he attacks you, a woman, because he is afraid to challenge my brother."

Alexis gave a little laugh and shook her head. "I can't picture Carlo angry."

"It takes a great deal to anger him," Bianca admitted, "but do not be misled," she warned. "He is capable of tremendous anger."

"I'll remember that," breathed Alexis fervently.

A ripple of applause washed through the house, gaining in intensity as the conductor reached the podium. He briefly acknowledged the audience, and then raised his baton. Alexis felt excitement knot her stomach, and clasped her hands tightly together. In only a few minutes she would at last hear Carlo perform.

The overture ended, and slowly the immense curtains slid apart, revealing the stage. Alexis hardly noticed the elaborate set, so intent was she on searching the stage for that one familiar figure.

At last she located him, seated downstage right, at an ornate writing desk, while the chorus sang upstage of him. The action of the opera continued as Oscar, page to King Ricardo, whom Carlo portrayed, presented his master with a list of ladies who would be present at the court ball. Among the names was that of Amelia, a married woman who was the love of Ricardo's life.

At this point Alexis leaned forward with anticipation, for Carlo was to sing his first solo aria. She had heard him in the library, accompanied only by a piano. Now his beautiful voice would have the support of a full orchestra, and of a house designed so that the sound would soar rather than be trapped, as it was in a small room.

He began to sing, and the audience became totally silent as the sounds fell before them. Alexis had spent part of the afternoon with Ian, reading over the libretto of the opera so she would understand most of the arias, or at any rate the ones Carlo sang. Now she found she really didn't need the translation. Carlo's face and tone were so expressive that she could feel the depth of his passion for Amelia, and the anguish and guilt he felt for loving her.

Alexis was shaken with the power and beauty of his voice, but also with the knowledge that she had somehow touched this amazing man, and that in some fashion he cared for her. The stage blurred before her as her eyes filled with tears. Embarrassed, she dabbed surreptitiously at the corners of her eyes with a fingertip. She prayed no one would notice her emotionalism, for it was impossible for her to explain why she was crying. It went beyond the beauty of the music. Somehow it was bound up in her desperate confusion over the singer. She drew in a deep breath and returned her attention to the stage, where the court was preparing to visit Ulrica, the sorceress, and where Carlo would hear the fatal prophecy fortelling his death.

The evening passed in a wonder of music, pageantry, and a never-ending line of people who came to speak with the Benonis during the intermissions.

Alexis' attention was riveted on the stage, waiting for the curtain to rise once more, when she was startled by someone possessively grasping her hand and pressing an ardent kiss onto the palm.

"I beg your pardon," she said, icily pulling her hand free.

The handsome young man who had kissed her hand, clutched melodramatically at his heart and took a feeble step backward.

"Ah, Bianca, you did not tell me she was cruel as well as beautiful."

Alexis looked in bewilderment from the stranger to Bianca and back again.

Bianca began to laugh. "Poor dear. Alexis, we are

teasing you, of course, but you must admit you haven't been very attentive. I introduced you to Ovidio, but I don't think you heard."

Alexis felt her cheeks grow warm and hung her head with mortification. It was true; she hadn't been paying attention to anyone who'd been introduced to her during the intermissions. She had just been waiting impatiently to see Carlo again.

"I'm sorry. Shall we try it again?" She smiled and held out her hand.

"I am Count Ovidio del Bracchio. Bianca told me of her charming American houseguest when she was in Naples, and I was determined to meet you."

"It's very nice to meet you, but I'm not really a houseguest. I'm here planning Signor Benoni's American tour."

"My, brains as well as beauty."

Embarrassed by the effusive count, and somewhat put off by his condescension, Alexis glanced down at her program, pretending to scan the synopsis of the final act.

The young Italian, apparently not sensing her mood, hung over the back of her chair and asked, "Do you like our country?"

"Very much. I was here years ago, but I was only a child, and I don't remember much."

"You are still only a child," he murmured huskily.

Alexis laughed at his absurd attempt to flirt, comparing it with Carlo's expertise. She swiveled around in her chair to better study the classic features of the count. In his dark way he was certainly as handsome as Michael had been, but he left her cold.

In spite of Ovidio's practiced sensuality, she found Carlo's magnetism to be far greater. The raw power of the singer radiated constantly from him. He had no need to turn it on, as this young man apparently did.

"I've been warned never to take any of you Italians

seriously," she replied lightly, and they spent the remainder of the intermission in trivial conversation.

There were thirteen curtain calls before the audience was satisfied and the curtain at last remained closed. Alexis was in such a daze that Bianca had to give her arm a gentle shake before she would move.

"Come, we're going to Carlo's dressing room."

Outside the box they found Ovidio waiting. "Do you mind if I join you?" he asked with an ingratiating smile. Bianca nodded her consent, and soon they were pushing through the milling crowds, all eagerly hurrying away to a late supper or gay party.

There was an enormous group of people clustered about the door of Carlo's dressing room, spilling and overflowing into the hall.

Carlo towered over most in the crowd, which, Alexis noticed with a pang, was predominantely female. And what an assemblage of females! Diamonds glittered at delicate earlobes, and she knew that the cost of any one of the gowns would keep her easily for a month. Greetings and compliments were called in numerous languages, with Carlo responding easily in most. It was a wealthy, glittering cosmopolitan crowd, and Alexis felt small and provincial. She wondered what Carlo could possibly see in her after being surrounded by the beauties of two continents. She started to retreat, but suddenly Carlo spied her, and pushed politely but inexorably through the crush to her side. Seizing her hand, he pressed a kiss first onto the back and then the palm. Even through the glove she could feel the warmth of his lips, and she felt a responding warmth growing in the core of her. There was a startled murmur from the throng, and more than a few jealous looks were directed toward Alexis.

She lifted her eyes to his sweat-damp face. The heavy makeup was streaked, leaving bold black slashes about his incredible eyes, and staining the collar of his costume. He looked tired, but his eyes were bright, as he absorbed the excitement of the evening and the adoration of his fans.

"I wanted to—" Alexis began.

"Later," he said in an undertone. "Tell me later, when we can be alone together." She subsided, happy in the knowledge that after the crowds were left behind he would be with her.

Ovidio pushed to Carlo's side and clapped him firmly on the shoulder. "It was magnificent, as usual, my friend."

"What is this scoundrel doing here?" Carlo called to Bianca over the babble of the throng. "I told you to guard my treasure," he reproved his sister, "and now I find you have let this blackguard near her. Did he make advances to my lady?"

"But of course. You can't have them all to yourself, Carlo." The young nobleman laughed.

"Why not?" Carlo boomed exuberantly, indicating with a sweep of his free arm that he would like to enfold all the assembled women. Alexis felt a stab of jealousy, for his actions seemed to offset his earlier words, but she tried to ignore it. After all, she reminded herself, she had spent the entire day trying to convince herself she and Carlo were only sharing a mild flirtation.

Twenty minutes later Gunther arrived, and dismissed the well-wishers and autograph seekers with curt gestures and clipped commands. Soon only a few immediate friends of the family's and Bianca and Alexis remained. Gunther had herded Carlo back into the dressing room to change.

"Where are your mother and Ian?" Alexis asked, suddenly noticing their absence now that the crush had abated.

"They have gone on ahead to hold down the restaurant

for our celebration dinner. It is going to be quite a party. Ovidio will be coming, and the Almafis, and I think Mama invited the della Rosas as well."

Alexis remained silent for several moments, carefully weighing her words. She didn't want to offend her friend, who had become so precious to her over the past weeks, but on the other hand she desperately wanted to be alone to think over and to savor this evening.

"Bianca, please don't be angry with me, but I really want to go back to the hotel. These are all your friends, and you're going to want to speak Italian, and the fact that I don't, is going to put a damper on your party." She held up one shapely hand to forestall the objections she saw rising to Bianca's lips. "You have made me feel totally welcome, so it's not that. I just want a chance to mull over and cherish this evening."

"All right, but it does not make me happy." Bianca gave her a quick embrace. "You have had a steady diet of Benonis for the past few weeks. You probably do need a break."

"You're a dangerous diet, too," Alexis said, laughing. "If I don't watch it, I could get hooked."

"We are counting on that."

Alexis walked to the stage door, then paused and looked back toward the dressing room. Carlo was in there, and if she wanted, she could accompany him to the party and sit blissfully in the circle of his arms. The desire to remain was a stabbing pain, but she tore herself free of the spell and stepped out into the clamor of the Roman night. Events were hurtling forward, carrying her helplessly in their wake. She needed time to think.

It was nearly two in the morning when there came a gentle knock on her door. Startled, she drew her delicate, sea-green robe tighter about her and, leaving the window seat, crossed to the door.

"Who is it?"

"Carlo."

Her heart began to hammer, and she rested her forehead against the carved surface of the door to stem a momentary faintness that threatened to overcome her. With clumsy fingers she unlocked and opened the door. Carlo was leaning nonchalantly against the door frame, a champagne bottle in one hand, and two glasses in the other.

"I came to share a toast with you," he explained.

Silently she stepped aside for him to enter. Crossing to the dresser, he tore the foil from the bottle. Staring at his broad back, Alexis asked, "Do you mind that I didn't come tonight?"

He busied himself for several more minutes with the cork before answering. "I would like to have had you with me, but I understood."

"I appreciate that. You can't know how much."

"Someday I hope you will tell me." He handed her a glass brimming with the bubbling golden liquid. As she accepted the drink, their fingers met briefly, and an electric shock flew through her body.

A mounting tension gripped the muscles of her neck and back, and in an effort to ease them she paced to the window.

"You like how I sing?"

"I cried," she answered simply.

He crossed slowly toward her. "No one has ever said anything so beautiful to me before."

"I tried to tell you at the theater," Alexis said, "but you wouldn't let me."

"I know. I wanted it all for me, with no curious listeners." He was standing very near now, and the fresh scent of him washed seductively over her.

"I don't know what more to say. It was . . . well, unlike anything . . ."

"You need another drink," he said, rescuing her from floundering about. She waited nervously while he filled the glass and returned to her side. She gulped at the chilled champagne, as an unaccustomed warmth swept through her.

Carlo allowed one hand to stroke softly across her shoulders and down her back. "You are very stiff. Here, I will fix that." He placed his drink on the windowsill and set to work kneading at the knotted muscles.

Alexis swayed under his powerful ministrations. The massage sent waves of pleasure rippling through her body, and the champagne had added its own lovely tingle.

Carlo's hands slowed in their sensual rhythm, and she gave a little purr of pleasure. Gripping her shoulders, he turned her to face him. They were so close, she could feel the material of his shirt brushing against her breasts, so thinly protected by the delicate robe and gown. Even from this unintentional contact she could feel the sensitive nipples stiffening, and she blushed deeply.

Suddenly he crushed her into an embrace that was almost terrifying in its intensity. His mouth explored the sweet contours of hers, and a liquid fire flowed through her veins. Unable to withhold herself any longer from this man, she pressed her body against his large frame, twining her fingers in the black hair where it curled so appealingly at the nape of his neck.

Her kisses became breathless, as demanding as his, and he gave a deep-throated growl as his hands traced the slender lines of her body. She was swept into his arms and carried swiftly to the bed. Depositing her gently on the covers, he stretched out next to her, never stopping his caresses.

He lifted his head from the delicate hollow at the base of her throat and muttered huskily, "I should have done this weeks ago, at that damn festival."

"I wanted you too, but I was frightened and couldn't face it," she admitted.

"You must never be frightened of me again, my darling Alexis," he said as he deftly pulled loose the ties that held the gauzy robe together. "I will give you so much, my love." He slipped a hand inside her gown and began rubbing her nipple between thumb and forefinger. She moaned her pleasure.

Carlo dropped his dark head, his mouth tracing the line his hand had brought to tingling awareness. He caught the tip of her pink nipple between his teeth and brought it to a swelling fullness. She moaned again and arched toward him. Her hands clutched at him, seeking to bring him to her, but he resisted, intent upon raising her to the highest peak of pleasure she could know, before giving her release. His fingers parted, probed, and stroked until her body vibrated with need. His mouth touched her bosom, and between bites and kisses he murmured, "You will sell your agency and stay with me, and when we go to America for my tour, we will arrange for your personal things to be shipped home to us."

The words cut like icy knives, driving deep into her breast. She had worked so hard for the agency! It was a symbol of everything she had built in the months since her divorce, and now Carlo was callously ordering her to give it up. She felt herself go rigid as he continued to make plans for her life. She was no longer in the arms of Carlo Benoni, but rather with Michael, hearing him outline her days, taking all individuality from her. She had reclaimed her own personality by founding the agency, and now to be ordered to sell her dream was more than she could bear. Roughly she pulled from his embrace.

Confused, Carlo pushed himself to a sitting position on the wide bed. "Darling, what is it?"

She sat up, flinging her long hair out of her eyes.

"You certainly make a lot of assumptions!" Her voice caught on the tears that lumped painfully in her throat. "My little business may not seem like much to you," she said, sobbing, "but I worked hard for it. How dare you make me less important than you! I'm a person too, and my dreams count for something." The tears coursed, acid-hot, down her cheeks. Miserably, she covered her face with her hands, her shoulders shaking with the violence of her emotions.

"My darling, my treasure! I never meant to suggest that you weren't important. It's just that I assumed—"

"You always assume, all of you," she cried bitterly. "But you never bother to ask." He reached out, touching her hair diffidently. She flinched away from him and wiped furiously at her eyes. "Get out, please just get out! I trusted you, and I should have known better."

He rose and stood hesitantly over her where she huddled on the bed. His shirt was half open, revealing his broad chest, and his handsome face was creased with worry and hurt.

"Alexis," he began.

"Go on!" she almost shrieked, for she felt her resolve slipping away in the face of his reproachful eyes. Grabbing his suit jacket, he moved swiftly to the door and quietly let himself out. The door closed with heartbreaking finality.

Alexis stared at the blank surface for several moments, then gave a cry of despair. Leaping to her feet, she ran to the door and wrenched it open.

"Carlo," she whimpered, looking down the hallway. But he was gone.

Sobs wracked her as she returned to her tumbled bed. *He's gone, he's gone, he's gone,* pounded the dreadful litany as the room lightened with the coming dawn.

CHAPTER
Ten

ALEXIS MADE A notation in her book and realized with a sense of hollowness that she was almost finished. A few more days, and the job would be done and she could go home. One part of her longed for that moment, that flight back to safety, while another grieved at the thought of leaving Carlo without having made amends.

"Well, that's it for today," she said quietly as she gathered her materials without looking at the singer.

"Alexis." She paused halfway to the door. Carlo cleared his throat and swiveled around in his chair to gaze out the window, his back to her. "You... uh ... you like to stay for rehearsal, maybe?"

She hugged the books tightly against her suddenly

aching chest. This was the first overture he had made toward her in the two days since their return to Florence.

Answer him, answer him! her mind yammered. *It's a surrender,* taunted another part, and she couldn't force a sound past the constriction blocking her throat.

"Carlo," she finally whispered. He spun his chair back to face her, his attention riveted on her, awaiting her answer.

And Ian entered. The pianist seemed to sense instantly that his timing was terrible. Muttering apologies, he began to back out of the room, but it was too late. Alexis, her cheeks flaming with confusion, slipped past the Scotsman and fled the room, away from Carlo's compelling presence.

She had only placed one foot on the stairs when Bianca hurried out of the door from the kitchen area. She was carrying a large bowl filled with bread crumbs.

"Please, Alexis," she said impulsively. "Don't go to your room again."

"Bianca, I really think it's better if I do."

"Alexis, what ever happened between you and Carlo?" She paused, searching for words. "Well, never mind. That is your business, but I don't see why it should affect our friendship. It is a beautiful day out, and I have bread for the fish, so why don't you come with me?"

Looking at the younger woman's woebegone face, Alexis realized it wasn't fair to cut Bianca off just because she and Carlo had . . . She quickly stopped the thought, unable to face what had happened that terrible night in Rome. Even days later she was still filled with loss and desolation every time she remembered the closing of that door.

Shifting her books into one arm, Alexis leaned down and gave Bianca a quick hug. "It is a beautiful day, and I would love to come with you. Just let me dump this load."

After depositing her materials, Alexis hurried back down and joined Bianca. As they passed the closed doors of Carlo's library, they could hear the muffled piano and the sound of Carlo's voice. Alexis frowned and almost paused, for the singer's voice seemed taut and stretched, lacking that floating quality that had made him world-famous. She gripped her hands together, hoping she wasn't the cause of the obvious stress that filled Carlo's voice. She prayed the effect was just caused by the closed door.

Bianca gave her a curious look, and Alexis forced a smile back onto her lips. "Well, where's this fish pond of yours?"

"It is far back in the garden and screened by a grove of trees." They were out of the villa now, and walking down one of the gravel paths that meandered through the grounds. The music of the fountains accompanied their footfalls, and Alexis felt some of the tension ease out of her.

Bianca toyed with the chunks of bread, not looking at Alexis, then said, "We have always called this our place of tears."

"Why?" Alexis didn't really want to know the answer, but she couldn't prevent herself from asking the question.

"When Carlo and I were little, we used to come here whenever we were unhappy. We thought it was a magical place, and we used to pretend that no evil could reach us when we were safe here."

Alexis closed her eyes briefly, picturing a younger Carlo, with tousled hair and beardless cheeks but the same beautiful eyes, fleeing to this garden refuge. She wondered fleetingly if he had visited this sanctuary since his return from Rome, or if it didn't matter that much. That thought hurt, and she buried it swiftly.

They had reached a seemingly impenetrable wall of trees. Bianca reached up and pulled aside several branches, and there, in the midst of a circle of trees, rested a tiny, crystal-blue rock pool. The grass, browning now with the onset of winter, grew to the edge of the water.

"It's lovely, but this isn't man-made, is it?"

"No, it is natural, unlike almost everything else in the garden. Come, let us sit and feed the fishes."

Alexis dropped onto the thick carpet of grass and looked into the blue depths of the pool. Quicksilver goldfish darted through the depths, rising to the surface in anticipation of food.

"Now, you can't tell me they're natural." She laughed.

"No," Bianca admitted. "Carlo and I brought our goldfish here one day and set them free. Amazingly, they have lived, and keep multiplying." The Italian woman placed the bowl between them, and they tossed crumbs to the greedy fish.

"Carlo told me you are nearing the end of your work here."

"Yes, that's true."

"I was thinking, then, that it might be pleasant if you and I went to Siena. It is the best-preserved medieval town in Italy, and every building is worth seeing."

Bianca's tone was innocent, but her head was down, and her shining black hair made an effective curtain, blocking her face.

Alexis was convinced she was about to be ensnared in another Benoni plot. She had not forgotten Bianca's "headaches" in Naples, and the calls she and Venezia had made that left Alexis alone with Carlo.

Throwing the remainder of her bread into the water, she knelt and grasped Bianca by the shoulders. The dark-haired girl looked up guiltily.

"Bianca, don't, please. I know what you're trying to do and I appreciate the thought, if not the action. But believe me, you'll only make things worse."

"I don't see how they could be worse," Bianca said sadly. "You and Carlo have quarreled, and soon you will be going home. I will miss you, Alexis. You are my friend."

"Oh, Bianca, you're my friend too. This doesn't mean we're not going to see each other again. You can come to America and visit me."

"I will come to visit you, but I had hoped you would be staying with us."

"That was silly, Bianca," Alexis replied, averting her head.

"But I have seen how Carlo looks at you!"

"Please, let's just drop it. I couldn't live with Carlo for three days even if he *had* asked me! He's much too domineering for me. I'm my own woman now, with my own business, and I won't be ordered about."

"Carlo is not what you think!" Bianca leaped to her feet and paced furiously away from Alexis. "The problem is not in Carlo; it is in you!"

Alexis stared numbly down at her hands. Everything was turning to ashes. First with Carlo, and now she had hurt and offended Bianca, who had shown her nothing but affection.

"Bianca, I'm sorry—"

"Alexis, I am sorry—"

They spoke together, then stopped and stared at each other.

"You first?"

Alexis shook her head. "No, we both know what we were going to say."

"Friends?"

"Friends." Alexis rose, shook out her skirt, and crossed to Bianca. They shook hands seriously, and then smiled.

"Will you come in now?" Bianca asked.

"No, I think I'll take a walk. I'll see you later, okay?"

"Si."

Bianca vanished through the wall of trees, sending a cascade of yellow leaves to the ground with her passing. A chill breeze hissed through the grass, and Alexis shivered at the mournful sound.

Had she been wrong to react the way she had in Rome? It had all been so wonderful, and now it was gone, and was she really the one to blame?

Her jaw tightened stubbornly. No, she hadn't overreacted; Carlo had assumed too much! Why did all the compromising have to come from her? He was so busy making plans. Why didn't those plans include his moving to America rather than her giving up everything and moving to Italy? He had always gotten his way, while she was just beginning to discover what it was like to make decisions for herself. No, she decided, she hadn't been wrong.

She clung to her sense of indignation, trying to tell herself that she did feel better, but deep inside there was a nagging sense that she *wasn't* right.

Her head had begun to ache. Pressing her fingertips against her temples, she sought to shut out everything, to stop thinking. Her room suddenly seemed very attractive, and she started for the house.

As she slipped in the front door, she noticed that the door of the library was slightly ajar. Alexis moved stealthily toward the staircase, hoping to pass by unnoticed.

"I tell you, you are being a fool." The voice was Gunther's. The anger seething from the room froze Alexis in place.

"It will not be the first time," came Carlo's mild reply.

"Carlo, we're not talking about your giving interviews in questionable taste, or being seen with three ladies on your arm. We are talking about your *career.*"

"Don't we always?"

"Damn it, I hate it when you become glib. America

cannot help your career. They will turn you into some media item, package and sell you like soap, and then drop you."

"But I'll make a lot of money before that happens, won't I? And I thought that was your primary interest as my business manager. After all, you're paid a percentage." The tone was still light, but Alexis thought she could detect a hint of steel in it.

"There comes a time when one must choose between art and profit."

"Oh, come now, Hans, that is simply too pompous. I think the basic problem is that you don't like Americans, and that I took—"

"You're right, I don't like them. And I should have thought that exposure to this travel agent would have taught you something about them as well."

"Gunther, I wouldn't continue with this if I were you." The tone was low and cold, the warning explicit. Alexis crept closer to the door, desperate to hear what they would say about her.

"Look at how she treats you. She has no subtlety or finesse. A European woman would know how to dally without tearing you and this household to pieces."

"Perhaps I am not interested in a dalliance."

"You must be joking! She is no one. A crass, forward American, but she has certainly handled you!"

"She is Ivan Dimitroff's daughter, which should be enough for anyone if they wish to trace her pedigree. But more important, she is herself. And now, since this is really none of your business, I think we should discuss Milan."

"Do you intend to take her to Milan? That would be disastrous. I trust you haven't forgotten . . ."

The manager's voice dropped beyond Alexis' hearing, and she inched forward, straining to hear. Gunther's voice was a low murmur rising and falling tantalizingly.

"That is over!" Carlo's roar was terrifying. Alexis fled toward the staircase, slipping on the marble-inlaid floor in her haste to escape. *"Over, over.* Push all you want, but it will make no difference! I will discuss this no more!"

Alexis ran up the stairs, her breath coming in sharp gasps, her heart hammering. She had never heard such a tone from Carlo. It was so ugly. Bleakly she wondered if they had still been discussing her, and if she had been the cause of the singer's fury.

She reached her room and slipped hastily inside. She sank onto the dressing-table chair and strove to stop the trembling of her knees.

If they had been talking about her, it served her right. After all, the eavesdropper deserved whatever she might hear. But it didn't fit somehow. She was convinced they had been talking of something or someone else. But who or what? And *what* was over? A tremor of dread shook her. She had the strongest sensation she was going to find out, and she wasn't at all certain she wanted to.

CHAPTER *Eleven*

"ALEXIS! I WILL speak with you!"

She gave a gasp of dismay and nearly dropped the delicate, filigreed-glass vase she was holding. She had managed to avoid Carlo, except for their work sessions, while at the villa. So how had he found her on a last shopping expedition in Florence?

Returning the vase to its place on the shelf, she turned slowly to face him. She quickly scanned his face for any sign of the anger that had possessed him the day before when she had overheard his conversation with Gunther, but all she saw was weariness and determination.

"Carlo, there are people here," she said in an undertone.

"At home you can escape into your room or my sister's

room. Here you must hear me out or make a scene." The teasing gleam that she knew so well had appeared in his compelling eyes. "Are you going to make a scene?"

"Of course not."

"Bene." A curious old Italian gentleman had been standing nearby and listening to their conversation with great interest. Carlo glanced from the old man to Alexis and back again. Then, with an irritated shrug, he took her elbow and pulled her behind some display shelves. The old man looked disappointed, then grinned broadly at Carlo and winked.

"You know, everyone in your country is crazy," announced Alexis, feeling some of her confidence returning, and trying to keep Carlo from discussing what seemed destined to be a serious topic.

"I am going to Pisa tomorrow," he said, ignoring her ruse. "I want you to be with me."

"W—will your mother and sister be coming?" She was furious at the small tremor that invaded her voice, and gave a quick cough.

"No. In a few days I must go to Milan for rehearsals and performances of *Bohème*. I want a vacation, and I want to spend it with you."

"Even... even after what happened in..." She gestured helplessly, unable to say anymore.

"That is one of the things we must settle. I will not allow you just to leave. I will not beg, Alexis; I am not that kind of man. But I think you know what it means to me to have you with me."

There it was. The challenge that had been so jokingly made weeks before had been reissued. It hung in the air between them and could not be ignored.

Alexis searched wildly for a means of escape. But there was no escape. This time she could not shift the responsibility to someone else. She had to make a decision.

She stole a look at him from beneath her long lashes. His gold-brown eyes were filled with hope and desire. His firm mouth beckoned her, and she realized that, more than anything, she wanted to feel his lips on hers. Studying his mobile, sensitive face, Alexis knew that if she accepted she would not be able to resist him. And she also knew that if she allowed her desire to rule, her future would become very much more complicated and uncertain than it was now.

She took one last desperate look about the shop, but there was no one to turn to. The answer had to come from within her. Slowly she nodded.

Carlo's whoop of delight caused the Italians to smile knowingly and the foreign visitors to look bewildered and ill at ease.

"You make your shopping," Carlo said, his English slipping in his excitement, "and I will make the packing." He started for the door, then turned back. *"Tesoro mio,* you will not be sorry, I promise."

A smattering of applause met his statement and his flourishing exit, and Alexis felt her cheeks burn. The man was impossible, she decided, and she wondered if he might not be too exhausting for a mortal woman. She returned to her shopping, but her mind was already in Pisa.

"Step lively, now," Carlo barked in a perfect imitation of a drill sergeant. "Breathe deeply. You only have two hundred steps to go, give or take a few."

"You're a sadist," Alexis panted. "Why aren't you winded?"

"I eat lots of pasta, drink plenty of wine, and I am a singer."

"I think you're just a big show-off."

He grinned at her and began to sing heartily as he marched up the stairs of the Leaning Tower of Pisa.

Alexis dropped back slightly to watch him, and to marvel at the change that had occurred in only one day. The drive to Pisa had been somewhat quiet, for Rome still hung between them. Then all at once, after they parked the car and had started to the tower, the tension had lifted. It was possible for them once again to have fun.

They finally reached the terrace at the top of the Leaning Tower. A cool breeze fanned Alexis' damp forehead. She didn't want to think about having to climb back down again.

"You are not afraid of heights, are you?"

"Fine time to ask. But no, I'm not."

"Good." Carlo beckoned. "Then come here and see the city."

If the height didn't bother her, Alexis had to admit that the tilt of the surface underfoot did. She was grateful when Carlo's arm pulled her securely against his side. They leaned over the iron railing and admired the view. Almost directly below were the cathedral and baptistery.

"How old are these buildings?" Alexis asked.

"The tower was begun in 1173 and completed in 1350. The cathedral, though, is nine hundred years old."

"It's hard to imagine, living, as I do, in a country that's only existed for two hundred years."

"Yes, and there is no doubt we have many ghosts," Carlo said seriously. Icy fingers seemed to crawl down Alexis' spine.

"Really?"

"Oh, yes," he answered gravely. "In fact, there is one now."

"Where?" Alexis' eyes quickly searched the terrace, but there was nothing to be seen except an elderly Japanese couple, heavily loaded down with cameras, and a bored American with his gushingly enthusiastic wife.

"That really *will* teach me to take you seriously," Alexis said, disgusted. "How—"

"Buono giorno, Signor Galileo." Carlo extended his hand, then looked embarrassed and quickly changed the half-completed handshake into a bow. "Not such a good day, you say?" He paused, nodding sagely, as if listening to a companion. "Oh, you would like all those people to get out of the way down there so you can drop those weights."

The Japanese couple was smiling and nodding, while the tiny, gray-haired husband unstrapped his camera. The bull-necked American had grasped his plump wife and was propelling her toward the stairs, casting hostile and suspicious glances at Carlo. His mouth was moving, but Alexis couldn't hear what he was saying. The giggles she'd been suppressing at last escaped, and she tottered away from the rail, whooping with laughter.

"Carlo, you nut! That man is probably going to report you, and we'll both be arrested."

"And if they tried to seize us, I would take you in my arms and we would fly from this place." He wrapped his arms about her waist and kissed her lightly on the top of the head. "You make me invincible. You are magic, my Alexis."

"S'cuse me, s'cuse me," said a voice behind them.

Carlo released Alexis and turned to face the hesitant man who had spoken. The Oriental gentleman bowed, and Carlo then bowed somewhat lower, at which point the Japanese bowed again, and Carlo returned the second bow.

"How do I stop this?" Carlo whispered in a desperate aside as he rose from his fifth bow.

"I don't know." Alexis chuckled.

"Some travel agent you are!"

At last Carlo grasped the man's hand and vigorously pumped it, preventing him from beginning another in the seemingly endless round of bows.

"You are Benoni, tra la la, yes?" He gestured with

a circular motion around his mouth, to indicate singing. His round face was wreathed in smiles, and he nodded until Alexis found herself joining in his head bobbing.

"*Si,* I am Benoni, tra la la."

"Make picture, please?"

"Of course, but you have to include my *fidanzata* as well, okay?" Carlo pulled Alexis to him, indicating that they were a package.

The little man nodded even harder to show his agreement.

"What does that mean?" Alexis asked suspiciously as she joined Carlo in front of one of the pillars.

"What, darling?"

"Fi . . . fida . . . well, whatever."

"Just a term of endearment," he answered blandly.

"Why don't I believe you when you look like that?" Alexis muttered almost under her breath.

The picture was quickly taken, and after more nods and bows were exchanged, the Japanese couple departed.

"Ready to go?" Carlo asked.

"I suppose we'd better; the sun is starting to set, and I don't want to try those stairs in the dark."

"We will go check in and rest, and then change for dinner."

Alexis felt her nerves tighten at the mention of a hotel. She was so nervous, she couldn't tell whether it was from anticipation or fear. Firmly she ordered herself to calm down and not look for trouble, as they started down the winding staircase.

At the Hotel Duomo she discovered that Carlo had already reserved separate rooms, and once more she was struck with his almost uncanny ability to read her moods and needs. He walked her to her room, then paused outside the door, holding her hands while the porter deposited her case in the room.

"My room is just down the hall, if you need me. I

will come for you in two hours for dinner. Is that all right?"

"Perfect. I'll be ready."

"I know. That is one of the things I love in you. You are always on time. *Arrivederci.*" He gave her hands one final squeeze and led the porter to his room. Alexis gave one last wave as he entered the room, and slowly closed her door.

She tried to rest but found herself too agitated. Giving up at last, she unpacked her case and began trying on outfits. She realized dismally that he'd seen everything she had, and puzzled over what she could do to liven up her tired dresses.

Gazing at the tumbled mess on the bed, Alexis was suddenly inspired. She slipped out of the long velvet skirt and lace blouse she'd worn in Naples and pulled on a calf-length white wool dress. To this unadorned base she added an embroidered belt stolen from a different outfit, and knotted a brightly colored scarf about her neck. A pair of high, soft brown boots completed the ensemble. Tortoiseshell combs held her ebony hair in the usual coil.

She studied the result, deciding that she liked it. It had a wild, adventurous, Cossack feel, and that was precisely how she felt tonight.

She had barely finished putting on her makeup, when Carlo knocked lightly on the door. Giving her nose one final pat of powder, she raced to the door and threw it open.

His teeth gleamed whitely against the dark of his beard as he laid an enormous bouquet of red roses across her arms.

She stared at them and struggled vainly for words. A mere thank you seemed so inadequate, and she was too shy to do what she longed to.

Carlo seemed to sense her confusion, and said, "I

have called room service, and they will come to place them in water. But before . . ." He pulled one perfect bud from its place among its fellows and deftly broke off the long stem. Reaching out, he nestled it among the dark masses of her hair.

Before withdrawing his hand, he allowed his long, tapering fingers to lightly trace the line of her cheek and jaw. She felt the pulse at the base of her throat beating to an ancient and primal need. She blushed at the desire that just the touch of his fingers had aroused. Slowly she stepped back from his powerful presence, and deposited the bouquet on the table near her bed. She smiled warmly as Carlo extended a hand, and she slipped hers confidently into his powerful grip.

"This restaurant is just off the Piazza del Duomo, where we were earlier. It has garden seating, and I think it will be pleasant," Carlo explained as they stepped out of the elevator.

After only a short walk, they were there. An obsequious headwaiter bowed them to their table, all the while maintaining a steady flow of comments to Carlo. The only phrase Alexis could understand was *"bella voce," "bella voce."* Beautiful voice. She smiled, realizing that even here Carlo couldn't escape the plaudits of his adoring fans. With a flourish, the waiter presented the menus to them and hurried away.

Gazing about, Alexis decided that "pleasant" had been an understatement. Delicate flickering lanterns of green and gold hung in the trees of the outdoor dining room. The lighted candles on each table reflected off gleaming crystal, linen, and china. To her left Alexis sensed rather than saw the looming presence of the Leaning Tower, hidden now in the darkness. Lifting her eyes over Carlo's dark head, she looked up at a sliver of a new moon. Venus, the morning star, hung trembling from the bottom point of the crescent.

"Do you know the story of Venus and the Moon?"

Carlo looked up from the menu. "That is what is known as a total non sequitur. What are you talking about?"

"Look behind you," Alexis ordered, pointing.

Carlo half turned in his chair and studied the unusual positioning of the planets. "All right, now I see the reason for the comment, and no, I do not know the story of Venus and the Moon."

"Legend has it," Alexis said, "that once, long ago, the Moon stole Venus's hair, but the gods have allowed her to try periodically to regain it. That is what she's doing now."

"I like that legend. But now I will tell you another story," Carlo said softly, capturing her hands with his. "Once there was a very lonely man—"

"Signor, signor!" It was their waiter who had returned with a pad and pen. Beaming, he presented them to Carlo. For an instant Carlo closed his eyes, but he quickly opened them and smiled up at the man as he accepted the paper and pen. The waiter and Carlo talked for a few moments; then Carlo dashed off a brief note.

Handing it back, he explained to Alexis, "It is for his daughter. He says she is in love with me, and that if she had learned he had served us tonight and had not gotten my autograph, he would not be able to live in his own home."

Alexis watched the man retreating happily with his prize and shook her head. "How do you deal with all the fame? Dad's well known within certain circles, but his life isn't the public whirl that yours is."

"It is very hard," Carlo responded seriously. "There are times when I think I can stand it no longer."

Startled, Alexis dropped her menu back onto the table. "That was meant to be a rhetorical question. I just assumed you loved it."

He shook his head, not looking at her. "All the adoration in the world cannot replace the sorrow of an empty home."

And neither can a career, thought Alexis suddenly, and the realization shook her.

"We are becoming melancholy," Carlo said, "but food and talk will cure that."

"And which is more important?" Alexis teased.

Carlo carefully considered the question. "Food. For without food, there is no strength to talk." He beckoned to their waiter. "But we also need something to loosen the tongue and make the talk flow. You have decided what you want?"

Alexis ordered the cannelloni. She had fallen in love with the northern Italian dish of delicate crepes wrapped about a filling of cheese and spinach, and she ordered it every chance she got. Carlo ordered the *trippa e zampa,* or tripe and calf's leg with sauce, as he translated for Alexis. She shuddered at his choice.

"You're too much of a carnivore for me."

"Meat and pasta make you strong." He thumped his chest vigorously with a fist. "You will drink some wine with me?"

"I'm going to have to if I'm to watch you eat that mess you've ordered."

Carlo's laugh filled the small garden. "I love your wit, Alexis."

"Is that what it is? Michael used to say it showed improper behavior on my part." Elation filled her. She had spoken of Michael, and for the first time that sense of freezing fear had not washed over her.

"This Michael sounds like a great fool," he said, shaking his head, his eyes watching her. "Charm and beauty, one can frequently find, but wit as well . . . A man should not shun such a gift." Gratefully she reached across the table, allowing his long fingers to wrap strongly about hers. She felt no need for words. She knew he understood and had accepted her unspoken thanks.

"Alexis, darling, why didn't you continue with your music? You have a great gift, you know. And do not give me this nonsense about not having enough discipline. When I first met you, I could accept that explanation, but now, after being with you, I know that is not true."

She averted her face and carefully examined the rough bark of the tree next to them, seeking time and answers. Slowly she said, "I guess I was afraid that if I really became successful I'd have to leave my father's protection. All I really ever wanted to do was to go from his guardianship into the care of my husband." She was shocked at the admission but knew it was true.

"But it didn't work, did it?" Carlo's voice was low, but his fingers increased their pressure, as if holding her in place until she had worked through this confession.

"No." Her answer was almost inaudible, even to her own ears.

"You know something, Alexis? I think you should go back to your music. I think if you do, you are going to find that part of you that is missing. You are a wonderful person—if you would only believe it."

She was saved from making any reply by the arrival of their meal, and she thankfully filled her mouth with a bite of the rich casserole.

"Is good?"

"Is *delizioso!*"

"Bravo! I think maybe you would like to learn my language, eh?"

She smiled across at him, thinking that for Carlo she would learn anything.

There was no further mention of serious matters. Instead they drank wine and flirted. Alexis was filled with a wild exhilaration that owed little to the alcohol.

Finishing the last sip of her coffee, she looked up to find his gold-flecked eyes devouring her.

"Would you like to go for a walk?" Carlo asked.

She shook her head, an emphatic gesture that sent her hair cascading about her shoulders.

"Oh, no!" She began to bundle it back into a smooth coil, when he caught her wrists.

"No! Leave it." He assisted her to her feet and rescued the rosebud from where it had fallen when her hair was released. Carefully he nestled it back into the silken mass. Satisfied with his handiwork, he slowly withdrew his hand, his fingers once more tracing the line of her cheek.

They didn't speak on the walk back to the hotel. He held only her hand, but the desire that flowed from him made her feel as if she were being embraced.

The elevator ride was too quickly over, and the door of her room loomed before her. Fear and anticipation warred within her, for now the decision rested with her. Rome flashed before her eyes—the passionate love play that had culminated in only a wrenching emptiness as she repulsed him. Would this be the same? They stopped before the door, their eyes locked. He didn't speak. He didn't have to. The question hung in the air between them. There was a brief vision of dark-blue eyes, but they fled before the onslaught of love and caring in Carlo's warm eyes. Smiling softly, Alexis opened the door and walked inside. Tossing her purse onto a chair, she spun and held out her arms to Carlo.

He closed the door and with a growl of desire swept her into his arms. His mouth covered her face with feverish kisses, as he worked to loosen her dress. The gown fell to the floor about her feet with a whisper of fabric, and, lifting her easily, he carried her to the bed. He undressed quickly, and at last she was able to caress the curling dark mat that covered his broad chest. From that first day in the vineyards she'd desired him and yet denied it. There could be no denial now.

His tongue explored the sweet cavity of her willing mouth, and her veins seemed filled with molten fire. His kisses became slower, more seductive, as he moved down her long neck to her delicate bosom. She moaned with pleasure and pulled him tightly against her.

His hands cupped her bosoms, his thumbs beginning a slow circular caress that sent stabs of delight deep into the core of her. Dropping his head, he kissed each rosy tip, bringing both to quivering tautness. His hands swept down her sides, leaving trails of fire, and gently caressed, then parted, her thighs. He seemed interested only in pleasuring her, with no thought to his own desires. Alexis found it breathtaking after Michael, who had simply conquered and used her. She began to explore his large frame, trying to give back to him some of the passion that filled her.

His hands continued their tantalizing play across her, and she arched desperately against his powerful body, yearning to be joined totally with him. The union, when it came, was shattering in its intensity. She cried aloud, and discovered that she was weeping.

She lay quietly with Carlo's cheek pressed against her breast as tears slipped slowly down her face.

"Oh, Alexis, my darling, my treasure. I love you." He took her face in both his hands, then felt the dampness left by her tears. "But why do you cry? I have not hurt you, have I?"

"No, Carlo, you could never hurt me."

"Then why do you weep?"

"Because I love you, and because I never thought I could love again, and you've given that back to me."

He settled himself more comfortably on the bed and pulled her head onto his shoulder. "Tell me, when did you first start to love me?"

"When you held me in your arms at the festival."

"It was much sooner for me. It was when you played for me. Ah, Alexis *mia*. What I saw in your eyes..." He paused to kiss her lightly. "What I saw was so sensitive and loving that I knew I wanted you to be my wife." He propped himself up on an elbow and gazed seriously down at her. "Will you, *mi amore?*"

Gently she brushed back a lock of black hair that fell over his eyes. Inwardly she was at peace. All doubts and fears had been removed.

"Si, mi amore. Oh, *si."*

"I love you too, Dad. I'll talk to you soon. Bye bye." Softly she replaced the receiver and smiled at Carlo, who straddled a nearby chair. The sleeves of his camel sweater were pushed back to the elbow, and his powerful arms rested lightly on the back of the chair.

"He is happy?" There was an anxious little frown between his upswept brows.

"Did you know," she said, not answering him, but rather crossing to him to run her hands through his dark hair, "that on the night I was born, my father called your father, and they decided to see us married?"

"What clever men," Carlo said with admiration. "But it was terrible of my father not to tell me what was in store for me. All these years of anticipation that were wasted. It could have been like a Renaissance betrothal," he said excitedly, warming to his subject. "Your papa could have sent me periodic pictures of you as you grew up, and then, when you at last came to marry me, I would have been mad with desire."

He leaped from the chair and crushed her against his massive form. His kiss was so demanding that it seemed to pull her very soul from her. She was totally one with Carlo. When at last he released her, she was weak and shaking with desire. She longed to sink down onto the thick carpet of the sitting room and pull him down to her. She ached for the touch of his hands on the curves of her body.

"Damn," he muttered as his hand traced the delicate lines of her face and neck, and he continued to place featherlike kisses on her eyes and temples. "I promised Hans I would work today." He heaved a sigh and reluctantly stepped away.

"That's all right. I have to call François and Amy."

"They are your friends in America, yes?"

"Friends and also business partners. I think they definitely need to be told and invited. They're my closest friends in the world—next to you, of course," she added softly.

"Then call, and I will try to survive until later."

"Me too," Alexis whispered, nibbling on his earlobe.

"Devil! Now, stop that, or I won't be able to leave."

Alexis laughed gaily and watched as he hurried from the room. She had just lifted the phone when Bianca rushed in.

"Ah, there you are. You must stop what you are doing and come." Her eyes were glowing with excitement.

"What's going on?" Alexis returned the receiver to its cradle.

"Mama has something for you."

"What have the two of you done?" she asked suspiciously as she followed the younger woman out of the room.

"Nothing dreadful, I promise. Just hurry and see."

Bianca led her upstairs to Venezia's bedroom. Their knock elicited a sleepy "*entrare*." Bianca pushed open the door, and Alexis stepped into sheer opulence.

Heavy blue drapes were drawn against the penetrating rays of the afternoon sun. A lush carpet of purest white lay underfoot. Alexis shuddered as she tried to imagine keeping it clean. Several comfortable chairs and a low divan covered in blue velvet were placed about the enormous room, and the wide bed was not hung with the traditional curtains and canopy; rather, the material had been draped to resemble a tent. It was a room from a thousand and one nights.

Venezia was reclining on the divan, a tea service and a tray of petit fours at hand. About her feet were four or five large trunks.

"Bene." She rose majestically from the couch, shaking out the folds of her elaborate, ivory-colored peignoir. She smiled warmly and kissed Alexis on both cheeks before dropping back onto the divan. "When you returned from Pisa yesterday with your news, Carlo was so exhausting, with his instructions and questions, that I simply had to flee and rest. But now I have gotten organized, and I have things for you."

She reached into one of the trunks and lifted out an armful of lace. Venezia gave the roll a deft flick, sending the snowflake-fine material cascading across the floor. Alexis estimated that there were at least twenty feet of the feathery substance, and she gave a gasp of wonder.

"It is a wedding veil, no? It is very old. Benoni brides have worn this for generations. I wore it, and it would please me if you would wear it. Someday maybe Bianca will wear it too—if she ever finds anyone." She cast a disapproving eye toward her unrepentent daughter.

"I would be honored," Alexis said simply.

"Show her the crown, Mama," Bianca urged.

"Oh, *sí."* Venezia pulled a small box out of a trunk and carefully unlocked it. Lifting the lid, she handed it to Alexis. Nestled in black velvet was a crown of orange blossoms, but the petals and leaves were carved out of various stones. Topaz, jade, and moonstone winked up at her.

"It is to hold the veil," Bianca explained.

"Couldn't I just hold it on with bobby pins?" Alexis asked faintly. "I'd be terrified to wear this."

"No, please, you must wear. Carlo wishes it." It was obvious from her tone that Venezia viewed Carlo's wishes as commands.

"Well—"

"Good!" Venezia hurried on, eager to avoid an exhausting dispute. "In this trunk is a wedding dress. Very old. I could not wear this dress, being larger than the lady for whom it was made, but I think you could. If you would rather have a new dress, I would understand, but if you like, you could try."

"How old is it?" Alexis looked back down at the jeweled flowers. The entire situation was beginning to take on a dreamlike quality.

"Two hundred years or more," Bianca answered. "It is made entirely from Florentine lace."

Two pair of eyes watched her expectantly. She shrugged helplessly and smiled. "How can I refuse?"

"Good, good. Now, out of those slacks," Bianca ordered. "You are going to become a fairy-tale princess."

With Venezia supervising and Bianca acting as lady's maid, Alexis was soon clothed in the antique dress. Bianca carefully placed the crown on Alexis' head, where it sparkled against the ebony of her hair. She draped the veil lightly over all, then critically straightened a fold.

"It's perfect," Venezia announced at last.

"Come and see." Bianca led Alexis to an enormous mirror, set in one corner of the room. Alexis gazed in awe at the vision in the glass. The square-cut neck emphasized the creamy line of her neck and bosom, and the skirt fell in soft, full folds from her tiny waist. The woman who looked back out of the reflection seemed a happy stranger to Alexis. For too long the eyes that had met hers when she looked into a mirror had been sad, tense, and frightened, but all that was gone now.

"I look like that Renaissance bride," she whispered.

"I beg your pardon?" Bianca asked, puzzled.

"Nothing, just a joke with Carlo."

"You love him very much, don't you?"

"With all my heart, Bianca. Everything is perfect now. Nothing could ever go wrong." The woman in the mirror smiled and nodded, but suddenly Alexis wondered if she was only a dream vision, destined to fade, as all dreams must fade.

CHAPTER
Twelve

"BUT CARLO, WE'RE so close to the end. Why not just go ahead and finish it?" Alexis leaned across the desk, staring down at the serenely smiling Benoni. Only yesterday she had been trying on a wedding dress and dreaming about how perfect he was, and here he was being totally exasperating.

"Alexis, love, I do not have to be in America until January, and it is only September. Soon we will be married, and we will have all those months to complete the itinerary. Besides, you will be with me in America, and can save me if I get into trouble." He smiled ingenuously up at her, and she felt her determination waver.

"You know," she said, moving around the desk to

curl up in his lap, "Gunther is right. You really are lazy."

"Don't be mean to me;" he complained. "Just because I would rather nuzzle you then select hotels." He gave her an ogling wink. "Besides, I need the relaxation."

"Oh, really? Why?"

"Have you forgotten already? And you call yourself a travel agent."

"What?"

"Tomorrow we must go to Milan."

"Oh, Carlo, I had forgotten. May I go to rehearsals with you this time?" She tugged playfully at his beard.

"You'll be bored."

"Not if I'm watching you."

"You say the nicest things. Yes, of course you may come to rehearsals with me. I hope that as long as I am singing, you will always be in the audience."

"And how am I going to take care of our children?"

"Hmmm. That is a problem, and one which I think we should devote hours of our time solving. Beginning right now." Gripping her tightly in his arms, he rose from the chair and deposited her on her feet. "Come, let us go for a walk. You can tell me all my faults. Somehow they sound very nice coming from your lips. Then, after you are finished, I will tell you how perfect you are."

"That will be a welcome change after Michael." Alexis laughed.

Carlo paused, striking his forehead with the heel of his hand. "I am an idiot. I must tell Ian that I do not feel like practicing today. *Momento*. I will be right back."

Alexis perched on the corner of the desk and shook her head over this crazy, wonderful man who had come to fill her life. Suddenly her eye was caught by an unopened envelope lying half hidden under a welter of papers.

The color was unusual, a pale silvery lavender, and the return address was printed in an elaborate script.

Yvonne Dupré, Paris, she read. Alexis wondered how many women Carlo had known. Many, she was sure, and most of them were probably far more elegant and sophisticated then she. Yet he had chosen her over all the other women in his fabulous life. Alexis hugged herself as if to remind her that it was real. She really was going to be Carlo Benoni's wife.

She glanced again at the envelope. The name was far larger than the return address and seemed to shout from the page, demanding attention. Alexis wondered what sort of woman this Yvonne Dupré was, and then decided with a sudden shiver that she really didn't want to know.

Outside, in the front hall, she heard Carlo shouting for her. Unconsciously she shoved the envelope beneath a pile of papers, as if hiding it, and joined the singer.

The next morning Alexis descended the stairs, lugging her suitcase. Bianca met her, dressed casually in boots and breeches and obviously prepared to ride.

"Why don't you ring for help?" the Italian woman scolded. "That is much too heavy for you to carry."

"I'm not used to servants," Alexis admitted sheepishly. "But what are you thinking of?" she asked seriously as she indicated Bianca's outfit. "We're leaving for Milan today."

"*You* are leaving for Milan today. Mama and I are staying home, so it will be just you, Carlo, and Gunther."

"The part about Carlo sounds lovely, but could we leave Gunther out of this?"

"Don't worry. I don't think he is eager to see you either. He left earlier with the car. Now, come and have some breakfast. Carlo is already at the table."

They walked arm in arm to the dining room. A broad smile crossed Carlo's face when he saw Alexis, and he paused in spreading marmalade to blow her a kiss.

"Well, I am for the stable, darlings. Have a wonderful

trip," Bianca said, bestowing a kiss on Carlo's cheek. "And hurry back to us."

Alexis accepted a cup of coffee and a croissant from the maid. "If you keep eating like that, you will fade away," Carlo remarked.

"Oh, I'm not concerned. There will always be enough of you to cover for me," she teased. "Are we riding in that red deathtrap of yours?"

"No, I made train reservations. That way we can kiss all the way to Milan."

"I'm surprised you didn't decide to try it while driving," Alexis replied dryly as she dusted the crumbs from her fingers and finished her coffee.

Old Agostino drove them to the station. Hailing a porter, they hurried through the crowded station and out onto the platform. Eight rails channeled into the great overarching dome of glass and steel which protected the trains and the travelers from the elements. Their train was already in, and after boarding, they pushed through the narrow hall to their compartment. Carlo pulled back the sliding door, allowing her to enter. Once the luggage was tucked away below the day couch, and the porter tipped, Carlo drew the curtains across the door.

Alexis stared out the window at the bustle on the platform, while Carlo removed his dark suit jacket and hat.

"I feel so mysterious and exotic," she confided to him over her shoulder. "I've only seen these first-class accommodations in the movies, and something exciting always happens to the people in them."

"That is quite true, and something exciting is about to happen to you right now. Come!" He held out his arms, and she came to him, reveling in his powerful maleness. In his arms she was safe, loved, and she never wanted to leave them. He pressed his mouth down on hers, his tongue probing and teasing with gentle caresses.

Her lips became hot beneath his kiss, and flames began to flicker in her veins.

A discreet knock brought them apart. Carlo opened the door and handed money to the porter, who carried in a magnum of champagne and glasses.

"Carlo, you're acting like this is our honeymoon," Alexis protested as he pulled the foil from the cork.

"I am just practicing. You see, I have never been on a honeymoon before, and I want to be sure that I do it perfectly."

"You're crazy! Just having you there would make it perfect."

He set aside the bottle and crossed to her; seizing both of her hands, he pressed kisses onto her palms. "You cannot know what it means to me to have you say such a thing." His eyes burned into hers, and a growing ache spread through her body.

"Alexis!" he cried suddenly. "What have I done?" He was staring thunderstruck at her right hand.

Worriedly she glanced down at the slender fingers where they rested in his. The hand seemed the same as ever, and with a frown she asked. "What do you mean?"

"I haven't bought you a ring!" The heel of his hand smacked firmly against his forehead. *"Idiota! Stupido! Asino!"* He paced furiously in the confines of the compartment.

"Carlo, Carlo." She caught him by the sleeve and pulled him down on to the couch. "It doesn't matter. I had all of that the first time, and never had love or happiness. Believe me, I'd far rather have your love and support than all the rings in the world."

"But I cannot even buy you one in Milan. Those bankers," he said with disgust. "Pah! They know nothing of romance. Their rings would be just hunks of rock without soul or poetry."

"Bankers," Alexis echoed. "You're a fine one to criticize bankers, you Florentine."

"Yes, but we were bankers with flair," he protested. "These cold, serious money-men bear no resemblance to the Medicis."

He sulked for a few moments, then brightened as a thought struck him. "Maybe this is for the best. We can have one designed. You and I will work on it together."

"That sounds perfect. Now forget the ring," she said firmly. "I want all your attention during the next few hours. Thinking of your rehearsing *Bohème* with some beautiful leading lady makes me jealous."

To her surprise, he didn't respond to her bantering. Instead a shadow passed over his face. Without answering, he pulled her against him, burying his face in her hair.

A finger of fear traced an icy line down her spine. He was hiding something, and she was terrified to discover what.

"Eh, *il grande* has arrived!" cried a stagehand perched precariously on the catwalk high above Carlo and Alexis' heads. Carlo beamed and waved at the stagehands and technical crew, who shouted greetings to him.

Alexis threw back her head and gazed up at the tangle of ropes and catwalks that rose ever higher into the shadowed vault of the immense backstage of the Teatro della Scala.

La Scala. She was in La Scala, and more than that, she had simply walked in the stage door with the world's most famous tenor. And he was her fiancé! She had been in many stage doors with her father but somehow had never felt quite this much excitement. She murmured a silent apology to her father, who was playing a concert in Brussels, but decided that it really was true. Singers just elicited more adoration than instrumentalists.

From the backstage area Carlo led her onto the great

bare stage, filled only with the sounds of hammers. She stepped toward the footlights and gazed out over the immense hall. Even in shadow, the gold of the great theater glistened, and Alexis could imagine what it was like when the chandeliers were brilliantly lit. From the orchestra level rose six tiers of seats.

"I can't imagine performing in a hall like this," she whispered to Carlo.

"You become accustomed to it, and the butterflies are the same anywhere—here or in someone's home."

"Do you get nervous?" Alexis asked, surprised.

"All the time."

Before they could continue their conversation, a handsome older man walked from the opposite wing. His dark hair was silver at the temples, and he wore his simple sweater and slacks the way many men would have worn a tuxedo. Alexis realized that this must be Rodolfo da Fabriano, the infamous and temperamental opera director. Reaching the couple, he smiled warmly and embraced Carlo, kissing him on both cheeks. Italian flew as the two men caught up on the months since they had last worked together. Alexis was content to wait, happy to watch the play of emotions across Carlo's beautiful face.

"But you have brought a guest," da Fabriano said, turning to Alexis.

"More than a guest; my *fidanzata*."

"So that's what it means!" Alexis blurted. "You told that little Japanese couple that I was your fiancée, and you hadn't even asked me!" She glared accusingly up at him.

Looking sheepishly down at his shoes, Carlo shrugged. "Well, I knew you were going to say yes. It was just a question of when."

"Such sublime arrogance." Rodolfo laughed. "He deserves to be jilted immediately."

"Well, I don't know if I'd go that far," Alexis responded quickly.

Carlo cleared his throat and continued with the introductions. "Rodolfo, if you have finished attacking my character, may I present Signorina Alexis Dimitroff."

"Ah, but I know your father. He must be very proud to have so lovely a daughter." She nodded slightly, acknowledging the compliment. The director turned back to Carlo. "Your fiancée, you said?"

"*Sí.*" Carlo's reply was terse as he gazed intently at da Fabriano.

"And you have . . ." The director gestured obscurely toward the front of the theater.

"All handled, I assure you."

"You relieve me. Now I must speak to Ettore. He insists on taking the waltz much too slowly. So pleased to meet you, signorina." He bowed elegantly over her hand. "Until later."

When they were alone, Alexis said, "I'd say that part about his being pleased to meet me isn't quite true. He seemed upset about something."

"Nonsense," Carlo responded, but there was a nervous edge to his voice.

They strolled to the dressing rooms, collecting people as they went. Costume designers, makeup coordinators, and other singers gathered about to chat or set up fittings. Carlo and Alexis had just reached his dressing room, when the street door was thrust open by a uniformed chauffeur, who stepped swiftly aside as a vibrant, dark beauty swept past. Her hair had been piled expertly on her head to emphasize the length of her creamy white throat. Dark mascara boldly outlined her cold black eyes. A fur-trimmed coat was slung casually over her shoulders, and her red wool dress clung to the lush curves of her body. Her eyes quickly searched the cluster of people about the dressing rooms until she found Carlo. She tossed the fur into the already overburdened arms of a maid who trailed silently after her.

"Carlo! *Amico mio!*"

Alexis stepped forward, curious to know who the woman was, but she also felt a tinge of foreboding. Before she could reach Carlo's side, her arm was caught by da Fabriano.

"Signorina, a moment of your time, please."

"But I should tell Carlo—"

"Do not worry. He will not miss you for a few minutes." Before she could protest further, the director had virtually hustled her out of the backstage area and onto the stage. He seemed to cast about, searching for something to say. Finally he asked, "How is your papa?"

"He . . . he's fine," Alexis answered, totally bewildered by da Fabriano's behavior.

A call from the rear of the house drew Fabriano's attention. "Please excuse me. I will return in a moment." He hurried away, and Alexis decided to find Carlo. It was clear to her that the director had nothing to say, and had only wanted to separate her from Carlo. Turning on her heel, she marched back to the dressing rooms. The crowd had dispersed, and Carlo was nowhere in sight.

Behind a door she heard a woman's low, passionate voice. A terrible dread squeezed Alexis' heart, and, grasping the handle, she opened the door.

Carlo and the dark-haired woman lay on a couch. Carlo's shirt was unbuttoned almost to his waist, and the woman was pressing fevered kisses onto his chest and throat. Her dress was pulled up to mid-thigh, and her legs twined about Carlo's as she lay atop him.

Alexis stared in disbelief at the scene, and a sob was torn from her throat. Carlo lifted his head and stared at her in horror as the color drained from his face. He struggled to free himself from the clinging arms of the woman.

Whirling, Alexis stumbled from the room. Behind her she could hear Carlo calling her name. She ignored him, and ran toward the stage door. Wrenching it open, she staggered onto the street, tears of agony and anger pouring down her cheeks.

The blow had been so sudden, so brutal, that she felt physically ill.

She had believed in him. Believed that she'd mattered to him. How could she have been such a fool as to think that she could ever attract and hold a man like Carlo Benoni? But why, why had he toyed with her so? She bit back a sob, realizing that people were staring curiously at her, and began to walk blindly.

A hand caught hers and swung her around. "Alexis, please, wait and listen," Carlo said. His hair was tousled. From the touch of *her* fingers, thought Alexis bitterly, and she jerked away from his hold.

"That woman, once we meant something to each other, but no more, at least not on my part. I wrote her weeks ago and told her it was over. Apparently she is not going to accept that easily."

Alexis laughed, a brittle, shattering sound. "Oh, yes, it really looked like it was over."

"She trapped me," he cried desperately. "Also, I must handle Yvonne just right, or there will be hell to pay."

Yvonne. Yvonne Dupré. Memory of the letter she'd seen washed over her. Carlo claimed that he had told her it was over, yet he was still receiving letters from her as late as yesterday, and was locked in her arms today. Tears stung her eyes at his deceit.

"Carlo, don't lie to me. Don't add that to everything else. Michael always treated me like a fool or a child, telling me anything he wanted. And I was stupid; I believed him. Well, I've learned a bit since then, and no man is going to make a fool of me again!"

She swiftly hailed a passing taxi, and before Carlo

could act, she had leaped in, ordering the driver to hurry. She sagged back against the seat, allowing the tears to come again.

A cold, hope-stealing lethargy had stolen over her body. It's over, one part of her whispered, yet another part could not bear the thought. Perhaps he had been telling the truth, she considered, as they pulled up before the hotel. Pulling a tissue from her purse, she wiped her eyes. During their time together Carlo had never lied to her. The circumstances were damning in this case, but perhaps they could be explained. Don't overreact, Alexis, she warned herself firmly as she paid the driver. Better to wait and talk with Carlo again, now that she was calmer.

A knock on the door sent her flying across the room. She had been trying vainly to read, and she flung the book heedlessly from her as she raced to answer his gentle rap. Seizing the knob, she pulled open the door.

"Car—" The greeting died in her throat. Yvonne Dupré smiled thinly and glided into the room.

"You should not have expected him, darling. Rodolfo still has him hard at work." Alexis could find nothing to say, and the dark beauty began prowling, catlike, around the room. She casually inspected Alexis' dresses, hung neatly in the closet, then crossed quickly to the connecting door.

Alexis made a small sound of protest. Yvonne's smile became even thinner at Alexis's distress, and slowly, almost languidly, she opened the door.

"But of course," she remarked after briefly surveying the adjoining room. "Connecting rooms. How coy, and how convenient. For him, of course," she added cruelly.

"What do you want here?" Alexis forced the words past the aching constriction in her throat.

"To talk to you, darling, of course. And to warn you.

Believe me," she purred, "I only have your best interests at heart."

"I'm sure of that," Alexis responded sarcastically. Dupré gave her a sharp look, as if reevaluating her opponent. Alexis was encouraged by even this small victory. In the hours since she'd left Carlo outside La Scala, she had thought long and hard about her reaction to this woman. She had realized that ever since her divorce she had been fleeing from ghosts, and now she wasn't about to allow a ghost from Carlo's past to come between them. Bad enough that hers had to intrude.

The Frenchwoman sank gracefully onto the small couch and invitingly patted the seat next to her. "Come sit beside me." Alexis remained stiffly in place, her back pressed firmly against the unyielding surface of the door, grateful for its support.

Yvonne shrugged elegantly. "As you wish. At any rate, I can see that you are a sweet and innocent young girl."

Alexis was faintly amused at the woman's assumption about her youth. She knew she looked younger than her twenty-eight years, and now she was pleased, for it had caused Yvonne Dupré to underestimate her. She smiled coldly, her green eyes glittering with anger, and said succinctly, "Don't count on it."

Icy black eyes met fiery green ones in a brief battle of wills. The French singer's eyes dropped first. This show of weakness seemed to infuriate her, for when she lifted her head once more, there was such malice on her white face that Alexis almost recoiled. In spite of her expression, the singer managed to keep her tone level, even pleasant.

"Let us try to keep this amiable—"

"Why?" Alexis interrupted. "We're enemies, and always will be. You want Carlo, but you can't have him, because he's mine now. I'm not about to deny my love for him, so I can't see that there's any point in continuing this conversation." She pulled open the door and stared significantly at Dupré.

"Go on, cackle, little hen," Yvonne hissed. "But you are a fool. I know my Carlo has wandered from me during our years together, but only briefly. It was I who discovered Carlo, and under my nurturing and tutelage he became what he is today. What we have is eternal, while you are only a diversion."

"I don't believe you," Alexis said. "People change. They want different things from life." Now that she was closer to the woman, Alexis could see that, in spite of her lush beauty, she was older than Carlo.

"Perhaps he might want you for a while, but your American charms will never keep him from me. To show you what I say is true, I have brought these." Reaching into her bag, the singer pulled out a sheaf of newspaper clippings. "These are only the English articles. I didn't bother with any others, for, since you are an American, I am quite certain you speak no other language than your own."

The Frenchwoman extended the bundle, and in spite of herself, Alexis took them. They spanned years, and all of the stories were the same—Benoni and Dupré. They were the beautiful couple of the continent. Their tempestuous fights and even more spectacular reconciliations were faithfully detailed in article after article.

Alexis felt very bland and provincial, and she began to wonder seriously why Carlo had proposed to her.

"Now you see, my darling. Why would Carlo settle for milk, when he has had champagne?"

"And I repeat," Alexis forced out, "people change. Maybe your time has passed." Her reply was pure bravado, but it hit the mark. Dupré winced, and Alexis realized that the other woman's age had become an obsession with her. She recovered quickly, however.

"I will tell you what, *petite*. We will put it to the test. I say to you that Carlo will always come to me when I call him, and nothing you can do or say will ever stop him."

"That's nonsense." But Alexis had to force the words past lips that suddenly seemed frozen.

"We shall see. I will be going now. Remember my words when he leaves you."

The singer swept past Alexis, filling her nostrils with the heavy, musky scent of her perfume, and the door clicked shut.

Alexis waited desperately through the hours for Carlo's return. It was obvious that Yvonne Dupré meant to try something, but what? And how could she be stopped? Carlo had said that Yvonne had to be handled right or she could make trouble. Alexis once more agitatedly paced the length of the room, twining her fingers together. What if Yvonne did something that caused a scandal and hurt Carlo?

There was a gentle knock on the door. She opened it more cautiously this time, but it was Carlo who waited in the hall.

He looked tired and worried, and Alexis found her anger melting away. She held out a hand to him, and he gripped it tightly.

"I am very hungry, but I will not go to eat unless you come with me."

"Well, we can't have you missing a meal," she teased gently. "Yes, let's go eat, and then we can talk."

They were both too emotionally drained by the day to contemplate leaving the hotel. Without touching each other, they walked through the lobby and into the elegant white-and-crystal dining room. Alexis stared silently at the menu and wondered how to approach the topic of the French singer. Carlo too seemed disinclined to talk, and kept his eyes on the print before him. They placed their orders and lapsed once more into silence.

"Yvonne Dupré came to see me today."

"Ah . . ." Carlo breathed and looked at her fearfully.

"She says you'll never give her up."

"That is utter nonsense. What we had is over. Surely you did not believe her."

"I tried not to, but I admit it wasn't easy when she showed me all those articles."

The skin above his beard turned a dull red, and he took a quick sip of water. "This gossip," he muttered with a dismissing gesture. "We are public people, so the public loves to feed on us. Alexis," he began, but was interrupted by the arrival of the headwaiter.

"*Telefono*, signor," he whispered to Carlo.

Carlo nodded then gripped Alexis' hand. "We will finish this when I return, and you will see that there is nothing to fear."

He was back in only a few moments. His eyes were dark with concern, and he fumbled for his wallet, saying, "It is Yvonne. She has collapsed and is in the hospital. She is calling for me," he concluded miserably.

Anger shot through her. "It's a trick, don't you see that!" Alexis whispered passionately. "She told me she was going to prove to me that you still loved her, and this is her way of doing it."

"I cannot believe that, and even if it is a trick, I must go to her."

"Then you *do* still love her!" Alexis accused.

"No, I do not! But I do feel affection for her, and I cannot just abandon her."

A painful ache spread through Alexis' breast. She fought to hold back the tears. "Are you going to go to her?"

"I must."

"Then don't expect to find me when you get back."

He froze in the act of withdrawing several bills from

his wallet. "We will discuss this when I return," he said, ignoring her ultimatum. He flung the money onto the table.

Alexis watched as he hurried from the restaurant. She longed to scream, to break the delicate crystal on the table, to run after him and force him to stay. But such behavior would never help. She had been betrayed, and only one course remained open to her—she would go home.

She had to hurry, though, for she had to be packed and gone before Carlo returned. She knew she must never see Carlo Benoni again, for she didn't think she could stand by her decision if she were once again in his magnetic presence.

CHAPTER
Thirteen

THE CLICK OF the latch brought her head up. She stiffened as the connecting door was pushed open, and she cursed herself for failing to lock it. Now it was too late. Carlo was in the room.

He looked hurt and miserable, and she longed to rush to him, to smooth back his dark hair. But that had been before. Viciously she quashed the treacherous thought and clung to her anger. Only in anger could she withstand him and escape.

His eyes widened as he surveyed the open case and the few dresses remaining to be packed. "Alexis, what are you doing?"

"I think that's fairly obvious," she shot sarcastically

at him. “I’m packing. I told you I was going to.” She turned from him and lifted the black velvet skirt she had worn in Naples. The memories flowed over her, and her hands trembled so that she could scarcely fold it.

“But why?” he asked, bewildered. She didn’t answer, just lifted her eyes and gazed at him bitterly. Suddenly he shook his head, as if clearing it. “Because I went to Yvonne? Is that why you are going?”

“How very astute of you!” Alexis said scornfully. Outrage filled her. “I guess you didn’t listen when I told you I’d leave if you went to her. How could I possibly stay here after what I’ve seen and heard today?”

“I tried to explain, but you wouldn’t listen!” He spread his hands helplessly.

“And why should I?” she retorted. “You’ve told me often enough never to take you seriously and that you Italians can’t be trusted.”

“I was just joking. Alexis, surely you’re not going to allow a few remarks made in jest to take control of your mind. Don’t be stupid.” The final words were low, almost inaudible, but Alexis heard them with painful clarity.

Don’t be an idiot. How can you be so stupid? Alexis, use your head. How many times during the almost three years of her marriage had she heard those comments? Too many to count. And in the face of them she had always retreated, confused, frightened, and unable to cope. But not this time! The vow taken in San Francisco became her sole focus, the only sure thing in a wildly shifting universe. She clung to it, allowing it to dominate, to fuel her anger. No one, *no one* was going to reduce her to the position of subservience that Michael had put her in.

Anger roiled through her. She was trembling with the force of it, and she clasped her hands tightly together, trying to calm herself at least to speak. She didn’t want him to see how raw and deep this wound went.

Carlo seemed to read her silence for a surrender. He smiled and crossed to the bed. Dropping down onto its soft surface, he looked up at her appealingly, a gleam in his gold-brown eyes.

"Of course you were right to be angry, my darling," he said soothingly. "I was a bad boy. I did have a rather long affair with Yvonne, but how was I to know that you were going to come into my life? If someone had told me, I would have waited for you." He grinned happily.

It would have worked before, that engaging Benoni grin that had crept inside, twining itself about her heart. Anger and pain stabbed through her, but she clenched her teeth with determination. It was too late for that. Too late for anything.

She raked him with cold eyes. "Tell me, how was dearest Yvonne?"

"She was feeling better. The doctors say it was exhaustion."

"A word covering a multitude of fictitious ailments," Alexis muttered scathingly.

"That was unworthy of you," Carlo said angrily. He closed his eyes, regaining control. "Alexis, listen. It is over with Yvonne."

"Then why did you go to her?"

"I had to, and not for the reasons you think, but out of duty and loyalty. We have shared much, and even though I no longer love her, I will not abandon her."

"So any time she needs you, you're just going to fly to her side, is that it?"

"No, I . . ." He hesitated.

"It's apparent to me that you will go. I must admit, though, you certainly have an interesting way of demonstrating your love. You run out on your fiancée, even though you know it's going to hurt her, so you can comfort your ex-mistress. If this is a taste of how you're going to treat your wife, I'm glad I missed out! I'm glad you *didn't* give me a ring, because it saves me the trouble of throwing it back at you now!" Her voice had risen, until she was almost shouting.

Something had been triggered in Carlo, however. A darkness seemed to settle over his eyes, and she saw a slow, heavy pulse beginning to hammer in his temple. The singer suddenly leaped from the bed and seized her shoulders with both hands. His fingers dug cruelly into her muscles, and Alexis felt her neck crack as he shook her wildly. His face was a mask of fury, and Alexis' anger faded before a growing fear at what she had unleashed.

"You have had quite a time with my character, based, apparently, upon what others have said to you and what you think you have seen. You would not listen to me or believe me, who loved you. Instead you turned back to your narrow, selfish little soul to accuse and to judge, without ever seeing anyone else's side! All right! You have had your say, and now you are going to hear me! I endured your rudeness and your anger, because I knew you had been hurt and because I believed that beneath that shell there was a very special person." His lips twisted in a sardonic mockery of a smile.

"So I worked and I was patient, believing that at the end I would have my love, and that she would be worth the effort. But I see now I was wrong!"

Alexis flinched from the force of his voice. She twisted in his viselike hold, seeking escape. But he wasn't finished with her yet. His voice dropped in volume, but it was all the more terrifying for its low coldness.

"What I have learned today is that beneath the shell there is no warm, loving woman. There is only a hateful, frightened child who could never return love, because she is so trapped in her own fears and suspicions."

Alexis staggered as he thrust her from him. His shoulders suddenly sagged as if his anger had drained all his strength from him. Slowly he turned and walked to the connecting door.

He placed one hand on the knob, then paused, his back to her. "Do you know how I spent the afternoon?" She struggled to answer but found she couldn't force a sound past her frozen lips. He shrugged and went on.

"I may as well tell you, for all the good it will do. I spent the afternoon firing Gunther and telling Rodolfo that I would not do *Bohème* with Yvonne."

The door opened and closed, and he was gone. The click of the lock was like a knife to her heart as Alexis realized what she had done. She had been duped by her own ugly suspicions and the malice of an evil and jealous woman. And now, as a result, she had lost the person most precious to her in all the world.

She raised trembling hands to cover her face. She longed to howl like some lost and wounded animal, and to run, to run wildly, blindly until she could run no longer. But there was no refuge to flee to. No safe place where all would be well. She was trapped forever with only herself.

Numbly she stared at the closed door and the neatly packed and waiting suitcase. She had no options left; home was her only refuge. She still had her business, after all. But she found no comfort in the cold, lonely thought. The only person who mattered would be here in Italy.

Desolation washed through her. Slowly she bent and picked up the case. Yes, she would go home.

Because there was no other place for Alexis Dimitroff to go.

No place.

CHAPTER *Fourteen*

"AH'M JUST SO thrilled with the trip you planned for us!" said Mrs. Pickford, a large woman in her mid-fifties. "Ah told Herbert that ah didn't want some ol' travel agent pushing us into a trip to one of those horrible heathen places where they don't even have the good sense to have their statues decently covered!" The older woman's lower lip trembled with indignation.

Alexis, seated behind her large mahogany desk in the inner office of World Seekers, struggled to keep her attention on Mrs. Pickford's inane comments. Upon her return from Italy, three days ago, she had thrown herself into work with a single-minded determination that left her friends bewildered and concerned.

With difficulty she pulled her mind back to the client

before her. "I'm certain England will be exactly wha you were looking for." Alexis forced a smile to her lip and, rising, extended one small hand to the woman "Thank you for allowing us to serve you."

She escorted Mrs. Pickford to the door of her smal office. Leaning wearily against the doorjamb, sh watched the Southerner sail past the front desks and ou the glass door into the cloudy San Francisco afternoon She caught François gazing intently at her, and to avoi even the unspoken interrogation from her friend, sh stepped quickly back into her office and shut the door She knew she couldn't continue to avoid her friend forever, but for now it was the only defense she had.

She drifted back to her desk and sank into the large leather-upholstered chair. Picking up Mrs. Pickford' check, she swiveled gently from side to side, studyin the large amount of money penned there. It represente success. It should make her happy. But it meant nothing Her life had narrowed to a dull, aching gray world with out laughter, joy, or love. She moved zombielike throug each day, trying to fill the emptiness with work.

With a sigh she let the narrow piece of paper flutte to the cluttered surface of her desk. Spinning away fron the desk, she rested her chin in one hand and stare dismally at a large, colorful poster advertising the glorie of the Greek islands.

"You're not showing much enthusiasm for tha check," chided a gentle voice. Startled, Alexis jerke back from her reverie to find Amy de Montmary perched elflike, on one corner of the desk.

"I didn't hear you come in."

"I knocked."

"Oh."

Silence fell between the two women. The tiny blond resolutely pushed her large, purple-framed glasses bac up onto her upturned nose and cleared her throat.

"Yes?" Alexis' unencouraging tone seemed to throw Amy into confusion.

"Um . . . um, I . . . brought in the mail." It obviously wasn't what she'd intended to say, but Alexis gave her no assistance. Amy's violet eyes mirrored hurt and worry, and Alexis felt ashamed at the way she was treating her best friend. The problem was that she didn't know how else to behave. If she opened even a little, she knew she wouldn't be able to control herself, and the whole miserable story would come pouring out. And that she couldn't bear. The wound was still too raw.

"Quite a haul, what?" Amy asked brightly as Alexis began sorting the stack. "Either we're doing something right," she continued, to fill the silence, "or all these countries are just dumping their unwanted brochures on us."

A long, ivory-colored envelope slipped from between two bright flyers to lie starkly against the dark green of Alexis' skirt. She stared transfixed at the achingly familiar stationery as an eerie sense of déjà vu overcame her.

"Oh, my," murmured Amy uncomfortably, seeing the return address. "Aren't you going to open it?" she added as Alexis picked up a pen from the desk.

"No, I'm going to return it." Her voice sounded dull and flat even to her own ears.

"Unopened! Alexis, you can't! I mean, besides being horribly rude on your part, he might need something."

"There are other travel agents."

"Maybe. But you took on the responsibility of his tour, and I think you should see it through."

"Are you saying that I'm being unprofessional?" cried Alexis, furiously throwing the pen back onto the desk. She knew she was overreacting, but her nerves were stretched so taut, she couldn't control the anger that swept through her.

Amy drew in a deep breath, then looked Alexis in the eye and stated bluntly, "Yes."

Such criticism from her best friend and her top agent stopped Alexis cold. Hanging her head, Alexis admitted that what she had been contemplating was wrong, but she dreaded what lay within the creamy envelope.

"Look, Alexis. I don't know what happened in Italy, but believe me, putting it off isn't going to make it any easier," Amy lectured.

"Right as usual, dear," she answered quietly, and, seizing a letter opener, slit the envelope. She didn't want to read what the letter might contain, but hope also ran tingling through her. Her trembling fingers reached into the envelope and met a folded sheet of paper. Hope blazed in her. He had written! She knew her joy was foolish—the letter might only contain anger and insults—but she couldn't shake the feeling that he would write, and somehow it would be all right. Freeing the note, she tossed the envelope aside and unfolded the paper. A check fluttered out onto the desk. The paper was blank.

Disconcerted, she lifted the check. The pretty floral pattern was unnervingly familiar—and with good reason, for the check was hers.

One of the first things she had done upon her return to San Francisco was to figure how much her being in Italy had cost Benoni. Arriving at a figure, she had gone to the bank and withdrawn that amount from her personal savings. The act had set her back dreadfully, but she didn't feel she could use the company's money, when the entire mess was solely her fault.

Her gesture in returning the money had been in the nature of an expiation, but now this had happened, and Alexis felt as if she had been slapped. An unreasoning rage tore through her. She leaped from her chair and stormed about the small room, while Amy looked on, amazed.

"How dare he? How dare he?" she choked out. "I sent him that money in good faith, and he responds by kicking me in the teeth! Isn't my money good enough for him?"

Amy shook her head helplessly, totally bewildered.

"Do you know what he did? Do you?" Alexis demanded.

"No; that's why I'm sitting here with my mouth hanging open. I can see that's a check, but so what? Didn't he owe you for your work?"

"No, he didn't owe me. I owed him, and that check was to pay him back."

"Oh, but—"

"I can see through him." Alexis spoke through gritted teeth, not allowing Amy to say a word. "This," she cried, shaking the check beneath Amy's nose, "this is just another example of how arrogant and overbearing he is. He's making the *grand* gesture." She made a sweeping, scornful bow. "Playing *il padrone* . . ." Her voice broke slightly as the memory of that magic night when Carlo had first carried her in his arms rushed over her. Furiously she shook away the tears, clinging to anger as her sole means of surviving the pain she felt.

"He doesn't need the money, but poor little Alexis does. Instead of treating me like a professional businesswoman, he reduces me to a . . . a . . ."

"What?"

"A courtesan!" Alexis cried, and burst into tears.

"Oh, baby, don't cry like this." Amy's arms were around her shoulders, stroking and soothing her. "You've always trusted me, ever since high school, so why not this time?"

"I can't, I can't. I'm so ashamed." Alexis groped her way back to her desk and pulled a tissue from the bottom drawer.

"Alexis, whatever you may have done or think you've done, it can't be *so* bad."

Alexis just nodded, continuing to weep.

"Alexis, what happened?" Amy's voice broke with alarm and sympathy. "You can't hold this inside forever. Please, what happened in Italy?"

Alexis' sobs had quieted to a low, desolate weeping. "I...I didn't do...what I went to do. I didn't finish the job!" she gasped miserably.

"I'm getting François," Amy stated, and, ignoring Alexis' protests, she hurried from the room. Soon the handsome Frenchman was there, enfolding her in his arms, patting and comforting her.

"Now, what is this mess?" he asked calmly, looking at his wife.

"Alexis says she didn't finish what she set out to do, but the way I look at it, Benoni's tour doesn't even start until January. It's not too late. She could go back and finish it."

Alexis' head snapped up at her friend's words. "No! I can't make that kind of a surrender!"

"Okay, that's fine," François said placatingly. "If your honor will not allow you to return, then you must simply forget it. That is the only way."

Forget. Forget the feel of his arms wrapped strongly about her body and the fire of his lips as they possessed her? And the laughter? God, how could she forget the laughter and the joy that had been theirs?

François suddenly held her at arm's length, gazing at her intently. "This has nothing to do with business, has it?" He rushed on without waiting for her reply. "I thought you were distressed because you thought you had jeopardized the company, but this is personal."

Alexis looked at the two dearest friends she had in the world and decided that continuing to lie accomplished nothing. She desperately needed someone to turn to, and she knew that her withdrawn silences had hurt her companions.

Pulling from François' hold, she walked slowly away, marshaling her thoughts. She turned to face them, deciding the direct approach was the best.

"I fell in love with him, and I agreed to marry him, but then it all just came apart." The brief little story hung baldly in the air between them. Stripped of the hurt and the passion, it seemed so pedestrian and boring, Alexis thought.

Amy sat amazed, but François looked at her shrewdly. He smiled as understanding dawned on his face. "And you still love him," he murmured.

"No, I don't!" Alexis said, tensely twining a tissue between her fingers. "He is an arrogant, overbearing Italian male, and I wouldn't have anything to do with him again."

"No, of course not, and that is why you are suffering the agonies of the damned. *Eh bien!* It is obvious. Either he is good enough for our Alexis or he is not. If he is worthy of her, then we must find a way to correct this tangle; and if not, we must help her to forget him."

Her office was beginning to take on a dreamlike quality, as she listened to François discuss her as if she weren't present. Suddenly the closeness of the small room was oppressive, and she felt imprisoned.

She hurried to her desk and groped for her handbag. "I . . . I'm sorry. I appreciate what you're trying to do, but please, please, leave me alone." Turning, she thrust past François, dodging his outstretched hand, and fled the office.

A quick cab ride, and she was home. She closed the door to her apartment, feeling safe within its familiar confines. Even though it was only four-thirty, she headed for her bedroom, determined to find oblivion in sleep.

As she passed the low coffee table in front of her Chinese-print sofa, she grabbed a recent issue of *Music Today*. She was so exhausted, and yet she had not been able to sleep. She hoped that reading the trade magazine for a while would help.

She creamed her face and hurried into a cozy old

flannel nightgown. Snuggling down beneath the covers, she propped the magazine on her knees and flipped casually through the pages. Suddenly a small headline leaped out at her.

Benoni Cancels.

Her eyes raced down the page. Over and over she scanned the brief article, as her mind refused to accept what she had read.

Trembling, she fell back against the pillows. Carlo had pulled out of the performance of *Bohème* at La Scala, and he had canceled all his concerts until further notice.

Tossing the magazine aside, she slipped from the bed and paced agitatedly around her bedroom. Why? Why had he done such a drastic thing? No matter how famous he was, this could only hurt him, so why?

She pulled to a halt as an agonizing thought struck her. What if he had married Yvonne? He would want to be with her, so maybe that was why he'd avoided all the performances. A gnawing pain settled in her chest as she considered the possibility.

After several minutes of analyzing the picture she had painted, Alexis had to reject it. It was totally unlike Carlo to renege on anything he'd agreed to do. If he had married, he would have waited until he had time to enjoy a honeymoon. There had to be another explanation.

Another picture formed, and this one felt right. Carlo, deeply, bitterly unhappy, unable to work, and without Gunther to nag and push him. A man who had retreated to the sanctuary of his home, refusing to come out.

A sudden chill shook Alexis, and she hurried back to the safety and warmth of her large, empty bed. Wrapping her arms about herself, she shivered under the blankets. She had spent many days in Carlo's company, and she knew that was how he would react. But who was the cause of the unhappiness? She faced it honestly and admitted that there could be no doubt. She was the reason for Carlo's retreat.

Numbly she stared at the rose-patterned wallpaper opposite the bed. With her eyes she carefully traced each leaf, the line of each petal, anything to avoid the inescapable. She was the reason that Carlo, considered by many to be the greatest tenor in the world, could not, or would not, sing.

She had humbled and diminished him, but the thought gave her no joy. Miserably she extinguished the light, allowing the room to fall into a darkness as black as that that filled her soul.

CHAPTER
Fifteen

TEETH CHATTERING, ALEXIS fumbled for her key, and at last got the door open. Her hair hung in wet tendrils all about her face, and her clothes were a clammy mess. She'd driven around Big Sur all day, seeking an answer to her dilemma, and had been caught in a dreadful rainstorm. Then she'd remembered that she hadn't had the convertible top on her car repaired before she'd left for Italy. It was jammed, and no amount of pulling, banging, or screaming could make it rise.

Leaving her shoes by the door, she pattered into the bathroom and quickly stripped off her wet things. She rubbed her nude body with a towel, then pulled on a fuzzy bathrobe and slippers.

Setting the kettle on the stove, she entered the living room and began to build a fire while waiting for the water to boil. She dropped down on the sheepskin rug before the hearth and tried again to reach a decision.

She could go back, she thought. It would be so easy. And Carlo had been so sweet about accepting her apology when she'd given him the broomstick. Maybe he'd act the same way if she returned to him after their terrible fight.

"And maybe he'll just rub your nose in it, and never let you forget, for the rest of your lives, how you crawled back to him," she said aloud.

Her pride and anger writhed up and choked the sad loneliness that had settled in her breast. The flames crackled in the fireplace, mirroring the hurt and anger that filled her soul. She stared into the fire, seeing Carlo's eyes reflected in the leaping flames. Resolutely she turned her back on the enticing vision. She had made her decision, and there was no turning back.

She crossed to the balcony and gazed, disgusted, at the clear, star-strewn sky. It was as if the storm had never happened. It had caused the temperature to plummet, however. Shivering, she closed the doors and returned to the fire. She glanced at the clock on the mantel, noting with surprise that it was already nine o'clock. She considered cooking a quick meal but decided that tea and bed were really more what she wanted.

She thoughtfully sipped the warm beverage and stared silently into the leaping flames; then, with a yawn, she rose, banked the fire, and padded into bed, where she fell straight to sleep.

"Libiamo ne' lieti calici che la bellezza infiora . . ."

Alexis struggled up from the depths of sleep. Grumbling, she reached for her clock radio, wondering why the silly thing had decided to go off at . . . She rubbed her eyes and blinked at the luminous numbers. 12:10.

"Libiamo ne' dolci fremiti . . ."

She frowned at the innocuous box, for the singing was continuing, but the radio was definitely not on. At last it penetrated her sleep-dulled mind. The voice was outside, and with it came the sounds of a small orchestra. Violin and cello, mostly, she automatically identified, with a bit of flute and clarinet thrown in.

Sleep fled as she sat bolt upright in bed. A nervous trembling seized her, and she clamped her teeth together to keep them from chattering. There was no voice in the world like the one lifted in song outside her apartment, and she knew she would have recognized that sound anywhere in the world.

Closing her eyes, she remembered that perfect drive from Pompeii to Rome, when Carlo had joked and teased her, threatening to serenade her beneath her hotel room. Well, he hadn't done it there; but now, incredibly, he was here, outside her apartment in San Francisco.

The Verdi aria was over, and Carlo launched into a love song from the *Barber of Seville*. The rich tones of his voice floated even through the tightly closed windows of her apartment.

"Oh, God," she whispered into the darkness. "What a fool I've been! I love him, and nothing else matters."

Carlo hadn't been the problem. The problem had been within her. She had allowed herself to become bitter and hateful after her experiences with Michael, and rather than make an effort to reach out, to touch, to love, she had been harsh and unyielding with men. If they stumbled at all or offended her in any way, she cut them out of her life.

She had known that her actions in Milan were wrong and unfair, but her stiff-necked pride was more important to her than her and Carlo's happiness. She had held an image of Michael constantly in her mind's eye, and she had superimposed this false vision over any man who came within her orbit. There was nothing of Michael in Carlo, and she had been a fool not to see it. She had been too small and mean to admit her mistake and go to him, but thank God, Carlo was stronger. He had swallowed his pride and come to her. For so proud and great a man to make such a sacrifice proved to her more than any words that he loved her.

She began giggling and, throwing back the covers, ran to the kitchen. Pots clattered onto the tile floor as she scrabbled in the cabinets for a large soup-pot. Clutching her prize, she quickly filled it with warm water; then, staggering a bit under the unwieldy load, she hurried to the balcony.

As she stepped up to the railing, she noticed that lights were going on up and down the street as Carlo continued his passionate aria. Windows banged up, and irate comments were shouted at the impervious Benoni.

"Hey, mister, you crazy, or what? Some of us are tryin' to sleep."

"Shut up, you clod," a young girl yelled from a window in the house across the street. "That's Carlo Benoni."

"I don't care if it's God Almighty; I just want him to shut up!"

By now Alexis was laughing so hard, she could hardly lift the pot onto the railing. Once it was secure on the narrow iron rim, she leaned over to gaze lovingly down at Carlo.

He and his small orchestra were well situated, beneath a streetlight. What a ham, she thought as she waved. His teeth gleamed whitely against the dark of his beard as he grinned and blew her a kiss, never missing a note in the aria.

Coyly she beckoned to him. He stepped closer, until he was almost directly beneath her. Alexis hefted the pot and poured the water over his dark head. His song ended with a squawk and a gasp as the cascade of water hit him.

"Devil!" he called, but he was laughing.

"Would you get up here before you get me evicted!" Alexis ordered.

"What are you going to meet me with at the door? A skillet?"

"You'll just have to come and see," she responded with a flirtatious toss of her head.

"I come," he said quickly. He hurried back to his orchestra and paid off everyone. The players were all very young—no doubt music students drawn from the local university, who would do a crazy thing for a few extra dollars.

Alexis became aware that her breath was misting in the air before her, that her feet were bare, and that her flimsy gown didn't leave much to the imagination. Blushing, she grabbed the empty soup-pot and retreated inside.

She paused to throw another log on the near-smoldering fire, then pulled a large towel from the linen closet. A quick rap on the door sent her flying to answer.

"So you meet me with a towel. Well, at least it is soft."

"Forget the towel," she responded, throwing it aside. "This is what I'm greeting you with." She wrapped her arms about his substantial form and lifted her lips to his. He didn't hestitate, but immediately captured them.

His warm tongue probed the sensitive recesses of her mouth, sending fire swelling and cascading through her body. She clung desperately to his powerful shoulders, pulling him to her. At last he released her, and Alexis stepped breathlessly back into the room, pulling him after her.

Retrieving the towel, she handed it to him. "Here, get dry, or you're going to catch your death."

He slipped out of his wet jacket and vigorously rubbed

his hair, never taking his eyes from her face.

"I had begun to fear that you really hated me, and that you were never going to come out. I couldn't sing without you, Alexis."

"I know," she said quietly.

"You knew, and yet you did not—"

"Oh, Carlo!" she cried. "I'm so ashamed. I knew you needed me, but I couldn't bring myself to admit that I was wrong. If you want to leave, I'll understand—"

"Ah, *il mio infante.*" He pulled her into his arms, pressing her against his damp shirt front. "This is no time for recriminations. I nearly lost you once. I won't allow what's happened to separate us again."

"Come over to the fire," she whispered against his ear.

As he sank down with her onto the soft sheepskin that lay before the dancing flames, he shot her a wicked look. "Don't you think I ought to take off these wet things?" His tone was innocent, but a devilish light glittered in his eyes.

The hot blood rushed from her bosom into her cheeks, but she met his gaze fearlessly, and languidly began to unbutton his shirt.

He reclined on the rug and allowed her to push the shirt off his powerful shoulders. She studied his broad chest, with its curling mat of black hair, then leaned forward and pressed her lips against the hollow of his throat, where a pulse beat strongly.

Turning his head, he nibbled on the soft skin of her lobe while his tongue darted in and out of her ear. She gave a gasp of pleasure, and her hands stroked down his sides. He growled deep in his throat and, pulling her to her feet, jerked the thin nightgown over her head. His clothes soon joined it in a heap on the floor, and the lovers dropped eagerly back onto the sheepskin.

The fire blazing in the hearth could not match the flames that devoured Alexis' body under Carlo's skillful hands. His lips left a burning trail as he explored her body. First her mouth, next a breast, then the gentle curve of her hip, and back to her mouth. She writhed against him, clutching his large form to her, begging for that ultimate oneness. Their joining, when it came, took them spiraling to that realm where there is no separation, only total commitment and love.

Sated and almost purring, Alexis nuzzled Carlo's shoulder, breathing in the powerful male scent of him. He slowly lifted his head to look at her.

"Tesoro mio," he whispered huskily. "That was utterly amazing." The love reflected in his eyes left Alexis shaken. Biting nervously at her lower lip, she searched for the words that would remove her burden of guilt.

"Carlo, I'm very sorry for the way I behaved. It was inexcusable. The only way I can explain it so that maybe you can forgive me is to—"

His lips descended ruthlessly upon hers, cutting her off in mid-word. For a moment she struggled, then gave herself over to the delicious sensation of Carlo's slow exploration of her mouth and neck. When she finally relaxed in his arms, he raised his head.

"You must not talk, explain, or apologize. I confronted Yvonne, and she told me what she said to you that day. No wonder you were so angry with me." He paused to brush with one finger over her eyebrows. "I understand. I understood almost from the first moment you came into my house. When I first saw you, I felt that the loveliest and most natural of women had entered my life. But I am no fool, Alexis. I could see you had been hurt and that you carried a great fear within you. You were like the sleeping princess surrounded by thorns, but these were thorns of your own cultivating, so I knew it was going to take time, care, and kindness to free you. But, my darling, never doubt that you were worth it."

Tears began to slide down her cheeks. "Oh, damn," she said, sniffling. "I seem to be making a habit of this."

He chuckled, pulling her to a sitting position. "Not to worry. But now you must stop your crying and listen to me."

The seriousness of his tone sent a tremor of dread through her. She gulped resolutely, trying to stem the steady flow of tears. He gently wiped away the drops with his thumbs, then held her at arm's length.

"Alexis, I ask you: are you free?"

Gazing into his sensitive face, she realized that there wasn't a hint of Michael's mocking, blue-eyed ghost, which she'd carried with her ever since her divorce. The gnawing fear that she'd lived with for so long was gone. Smiling tremulously, she held out one hand to him. "Yes, Carlo, oh, yes!"

"Good, but before I ask you *again* to marry me, I have one other matter to settle with you."

"Y—yes?"

"Do you promise you will never, ever again throw a bucket of water over my head?"

"It wasn't a bucket." She giggled. "It was only a potful."

"Not even a thimbleful," he warned, catching her chin in his hand.

She smiled and nodded, then pressed a kiss onto the palm of his hand.

"Good. Then, my darling, dearest Alexis, will you marry me?"

"Yes, Carlo, I will marry you."

As she snuggled drowsily into his arms, Alexis wondered if François and Amy would be willing to buy her share of the travel agency.

She had been helping others to discover the world, but now it was her turn. Together she and Carlo would explore all that life had to offer. And it would be a life filled with love and laughter and, above all, music.

WATCH FOR 6 NEW TITLES EVERY MONTH!

WATCH FOR
6 NEW TITLES EVERY MONTH!

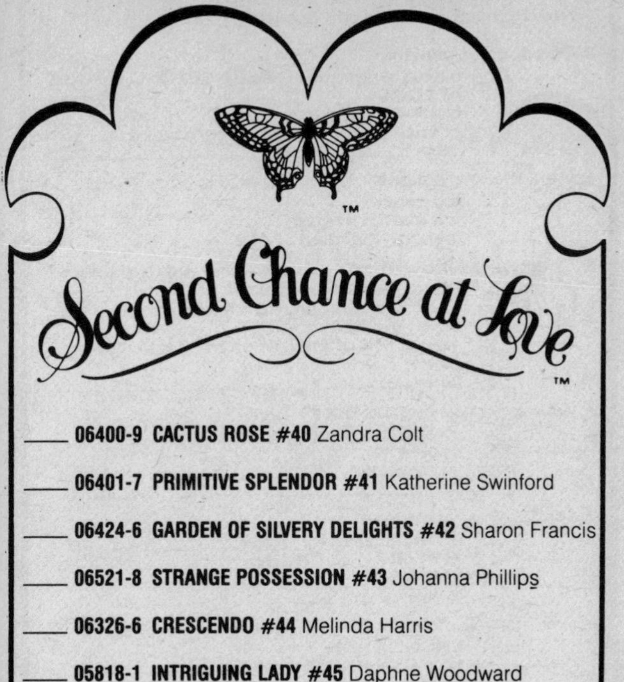

_____ **06400-9 CACTUS ROSE #40** Zandra Colt

_____ **06401-7 PRIMITIVE SPLENDOR #41** Katherine Swinford

_____ **06424-6 GARDEN OF SILVERY DELIGHTS #42** Sharon Francis

_____ **06521-8 STRANGE POSSESSION #43** Johanna Phillips

_____ **06326-6 CRESCENDO #44** Melinda Harris

_____ **05818-1 INTRIGUING LADY #45** Daphne Woodward

All titles $1.75

Available at your local bookstore or return this form to:

SECOND CHANCE AT LOVE
The Berkley/Jove Publishing Group
200 Madison Avenue, New York, New York 10016

Please enclose 50¢ for postage and handling for one book, 25¢ each add'l book ($1.25 max.). No cash, CODs or stamps. Total amount enclosed: $ __________ in check or money order.

NAME ______________________________

ADDRESS ______________________________

CITY ____________________ **STATE/ZIP** __________

Allow six weeks for delivery. **SK-41**

QUESTIONNAIRE

1. How many romances do you *read* each month? ______

2. How many of these do you *buy* each month? ______

3. Do you read primarily

☐ novels in romance lines like SECOND CHANCE AT LOVE
☐ historical romances
☐ bestselling contemporary romances
☐ other ______

4. Were the love scenes in this novel (this is book # ______)

☐ too explicit
☐ not explicit enough
☐ tastefully handled

5. On what basis do you make your decision to buy a romance?

☐ friend's recommendation
☐ bookseller's recommendation
☐ art on the front cover
☐ description of the plot on the back cover
☐ author
☐ other ______

6. Where did you buy this book?

☐ chain store (drug, department, etc.)
☐ bookstore
☐ supermarket
☐ other ______

7. Mind telling your age?

☐ under 18
☐ 18 to 30
☐ 31 to 45
☐ over 45

8. How many SECOND CHANCE AT LOVE novels have you read?

☐ this is the first
☐ some (give number, please ______)

9. How do you rate SECOND CHANCE AT LOVE vs. competing lines?

☐ poor
☐ fair
☐ good
☐ excellent

10. Check here if you would like to

☐ receive the SECOND CHANCE AT LOVE Newsletter

Fill-in your name and address below:

name: ______

street address: ______

city ______ state ______ zip ______

Please share your other ideas about romances with us on an additional sheet and attach it securely to this questionnaire.

PLEASE RETURN THIS QUESTIONNAIRE TO:
SECOND CHANCE AT LOVE, THE BERKLEY/JOVE PUBLISHING GROUP
200 Madison Avenue, New York, New York 10016